A Family Matter

The Will Eisner Library

from W. W. Norton & Company

Hardcover Compilations

The Contract With God *Trilogy: Life on Dropsie Avenue*
Will Eisner's New York: Life in the Big City
Life, in Pictures: Autobiographical Stories

Paperbacks

A Contract With God
A Life Force
Dropsie Avenue
New York: The Big City
City People Notebook
Will Eisner Reader
The Dreamer
Invisible People
To the Heart of the Storm
The Name of the Game
The Building
The Plot: The Secret Story of the Protocols of the Elders of Zion
Life on Another Planet
A Family Matter
Minor Miracles

Instructional Textbooks

Comics and Sequential Art
Graphic Storytelling and Visual Narrative
Expressive Anatomy for Comics and Narrative

Other Books by Will Eisner

Fagin the Jew
Last Day in Vietnam
Eisner/Miller
The Spirit Archives
Will Eisner Sketchbook
Will Eisner's Shop Talk
Hawks of the Seas
The Princess and the Frog
The Last Knight
Moby Dick
Sundiata

A FAMILY MATTER

Will Eisner

W. W. Norton & Company
New York • London

First published as a
Norton paperback 2009

For information about permission to reproduce
selections from this book, write to Permissions,
W. W. Norton & Company, Inc.,
500 Fifth Avenue, New York, NY 10110

For information about special discounts for bulk
purchases, please contact W. W. Norton Special Sales at
specialsales@wwnorton.com or 800-233-4830

Manufacturing by RR Donnelley, Willard
Production manager: Devon Zahn
Digital production manager: Joe Lops

Library of Congress Cataloging-in-Publication Data

Eisner, Will.
A family matter / Will Eisner.
p. cm.
Originally published: Northampton, MA :
Kitchen Sink Press, c1998.
ISBN 978-0-393-32813-4 (pbk.)
1. Graphic novels. I. Title.
PN6727.E4F36 2009
741.5'973—dc22
2009018004

W. W. Norton & Company, Inc.
500 Fifth Avenue, New York, N.Y. 10110
www.wwnorton.com

W. W. Norton & Company Ltd.
Castle House, 75/76 Wells Street,
London W1T 3QT

1 2 3 4 5 6 7 8 9 0

A Family Matter

THE FAMILY

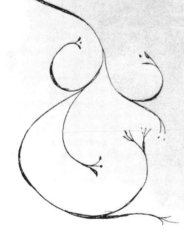

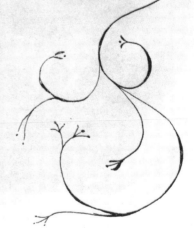

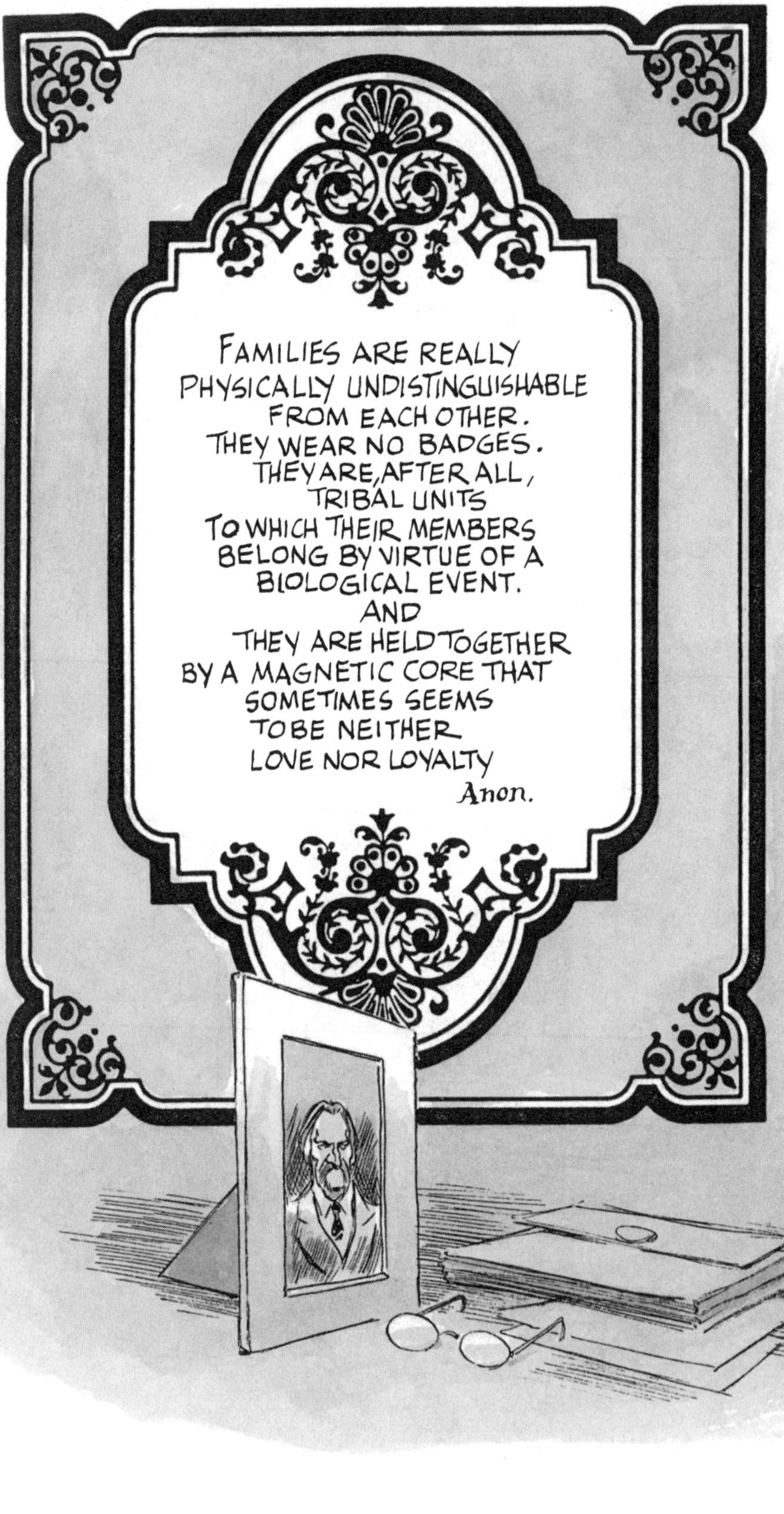
FAMILIES ARE REALLY
PHYSICALLY UNDISTINGUISHABLE
FROM EACH OTHER.
THEY WEAR NO BADGES.
THEY ARE, AFTER ALL,
TRIBAL UNITS
TO WHICH THEIR MEMBERS
BELONG BY VIRTUE OF A
BIOLOGICAL EVENT.
AND
THEY ARE HELD TOGETHER
BY A MAGNETIC CORE THAT
SOMETIMES SEEMS
TO BE NEITHER
LOVE NOR LOYALTY
Anon.

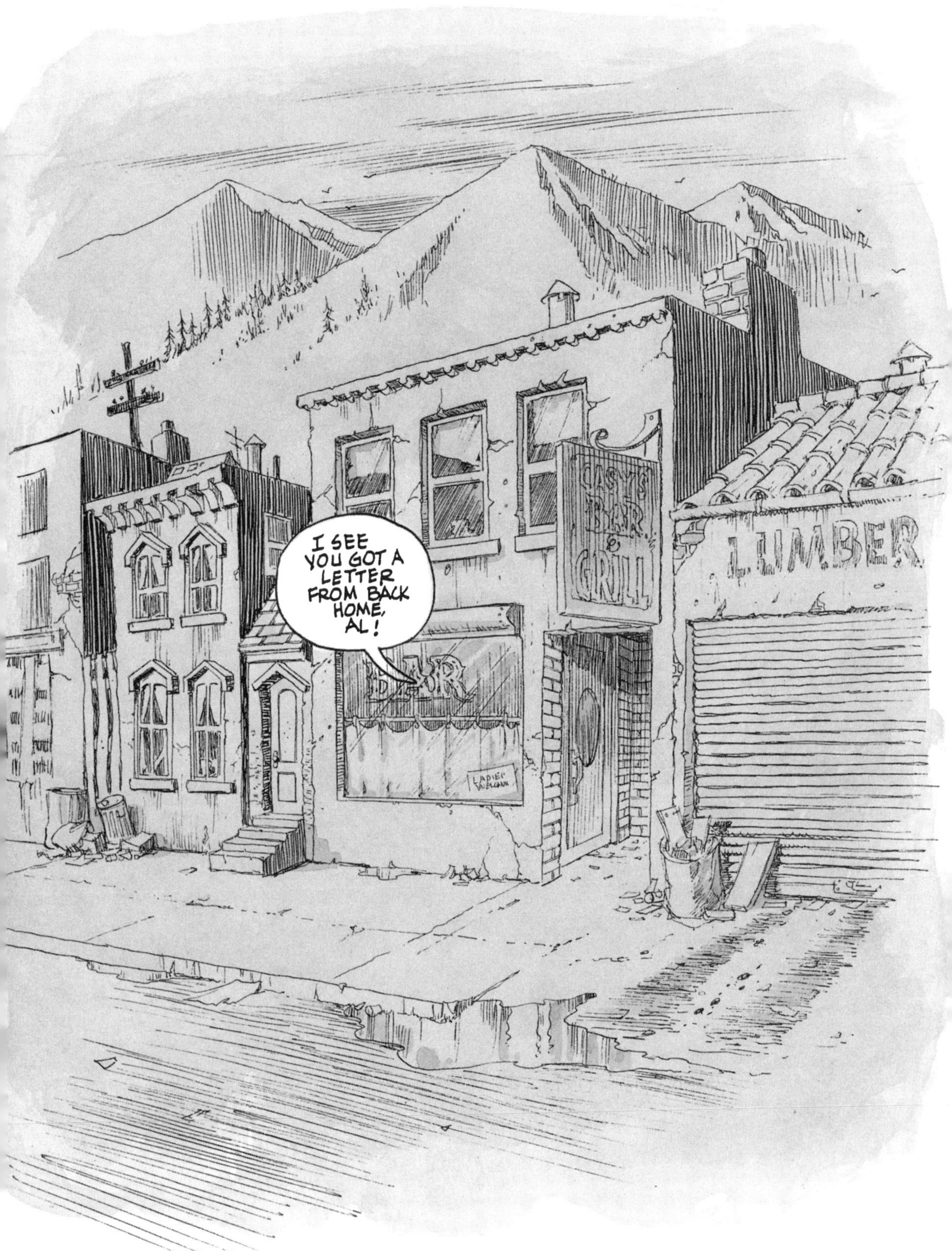
I SEE YOU GOT A LETTER FROM BACK HOME, AL!
CASY'S BAR & GRILL
LUMBER

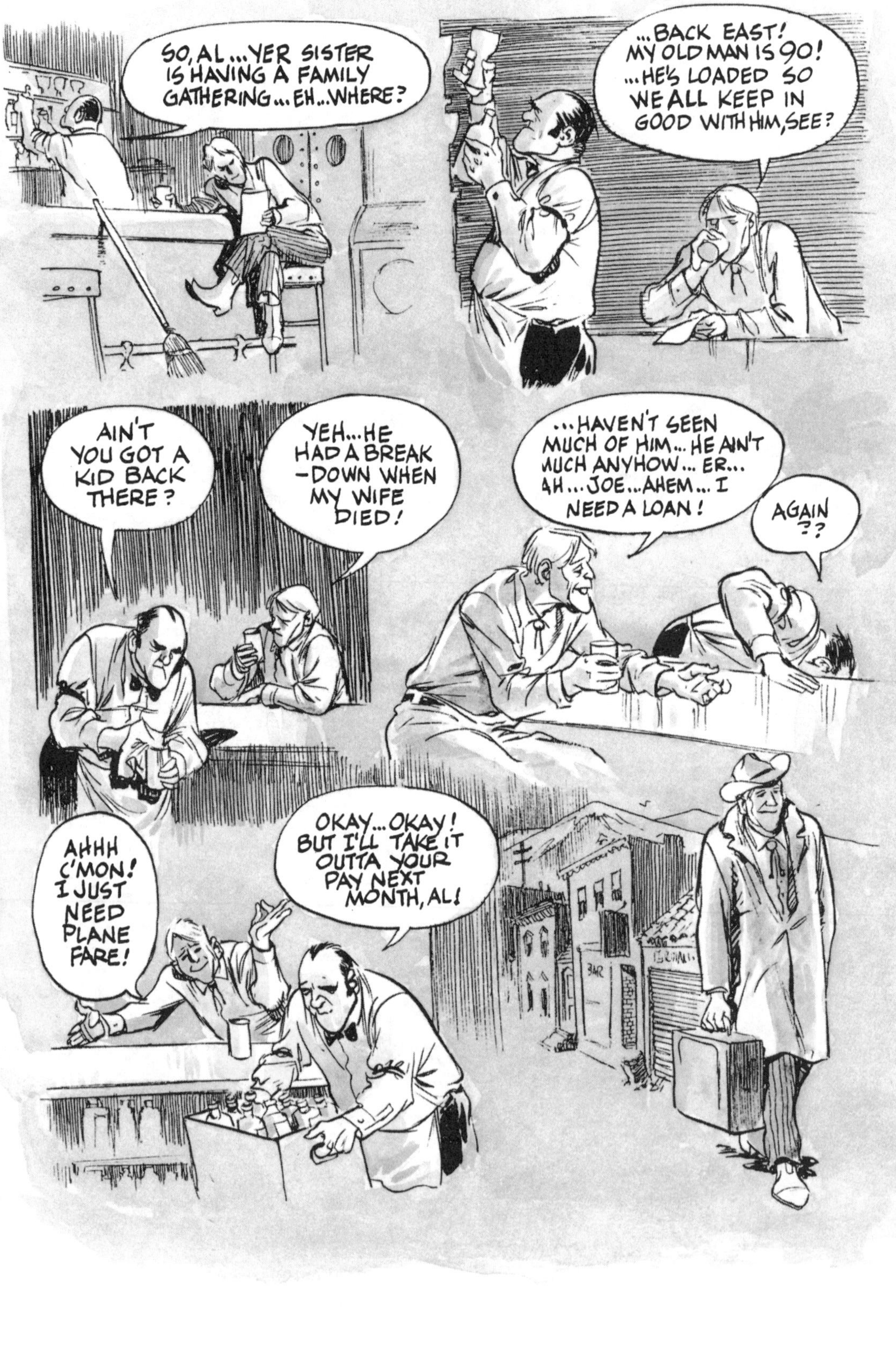
SO, AL...YER SISTER IS HAVING A FAMILY GATHERING...EH...WHERE?
...BACK EAST! MY OLD MAN IS 90! ...HE'S LOADED SO WE ALL KEEP IN GOOD WITH HIM, SEE?
AIN'T YOU GOT A KID BACK THERE?
YEH...HE HAD A BREAK-DOWN WHEN MY WIFE DIED!
...HAVEN'T SEEN MUCH OF HIM...HE AIN'T MUCH ANYHOW...ER... AH...JOE...AHEM...I NEED A LOAN!
AGAIN ??
AHHH C'MON! I JUST NEED PLANE FARE!
OKAY...OKAY! BUT I'LL TAKE IT OUTTA YOUR PAY NEXT MONTH, AL!
BAR

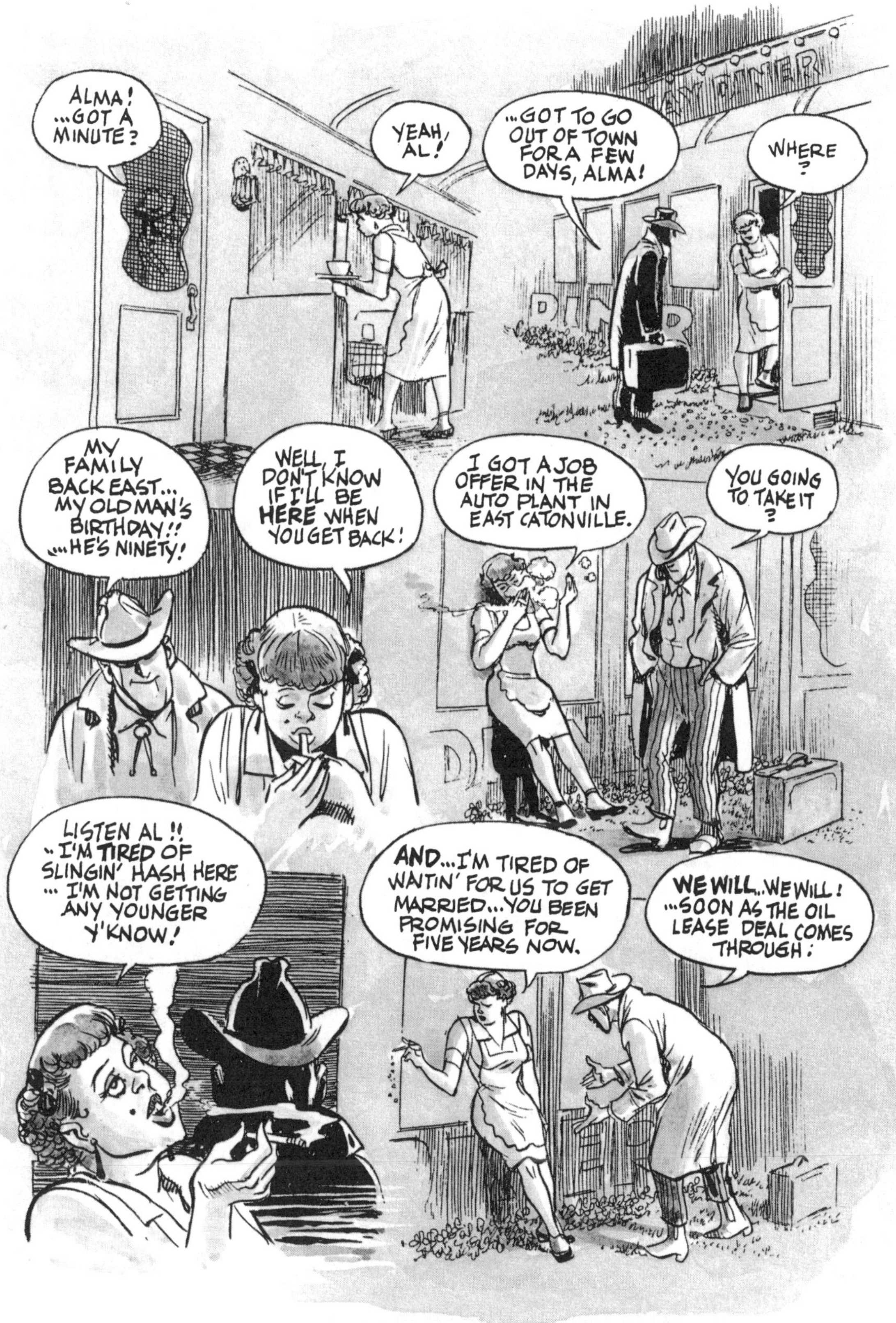

ALMA! ...GOT A MINUTE?
YEAH, AL!
...GOT TO GO OUT OF TOWN FOR A FEW DAYS, ALMA!
WHERE?
MY FAMILY BACK EAST... MY OLD MAN'S BIRTHDAY!! ...HE'S NINETY!
WELL, I DON'T KNOW IF I'LL BE HERE WHEN YOU GET BACK!
I GOT A JOB OFFER IN THE AUTO PLANT IN EAST CATONVILLE.
YOU GOING TO TAKE IT?
LISTEN AL!! ..I'M TIRED OF SLINGIN' HASH HERE ... I'M NOT GETTING ANY YOUNGER Y'KNOW!
AND...I'M TIRED OF WAITIN' FOR US TO GET MARRIED...YOU BEEN PROMISING FOR FIVE YEARS NOW.
WE WILL..WE WILL! ...SOON AS THE OIL LEASE DEAL COMES THROUGH:

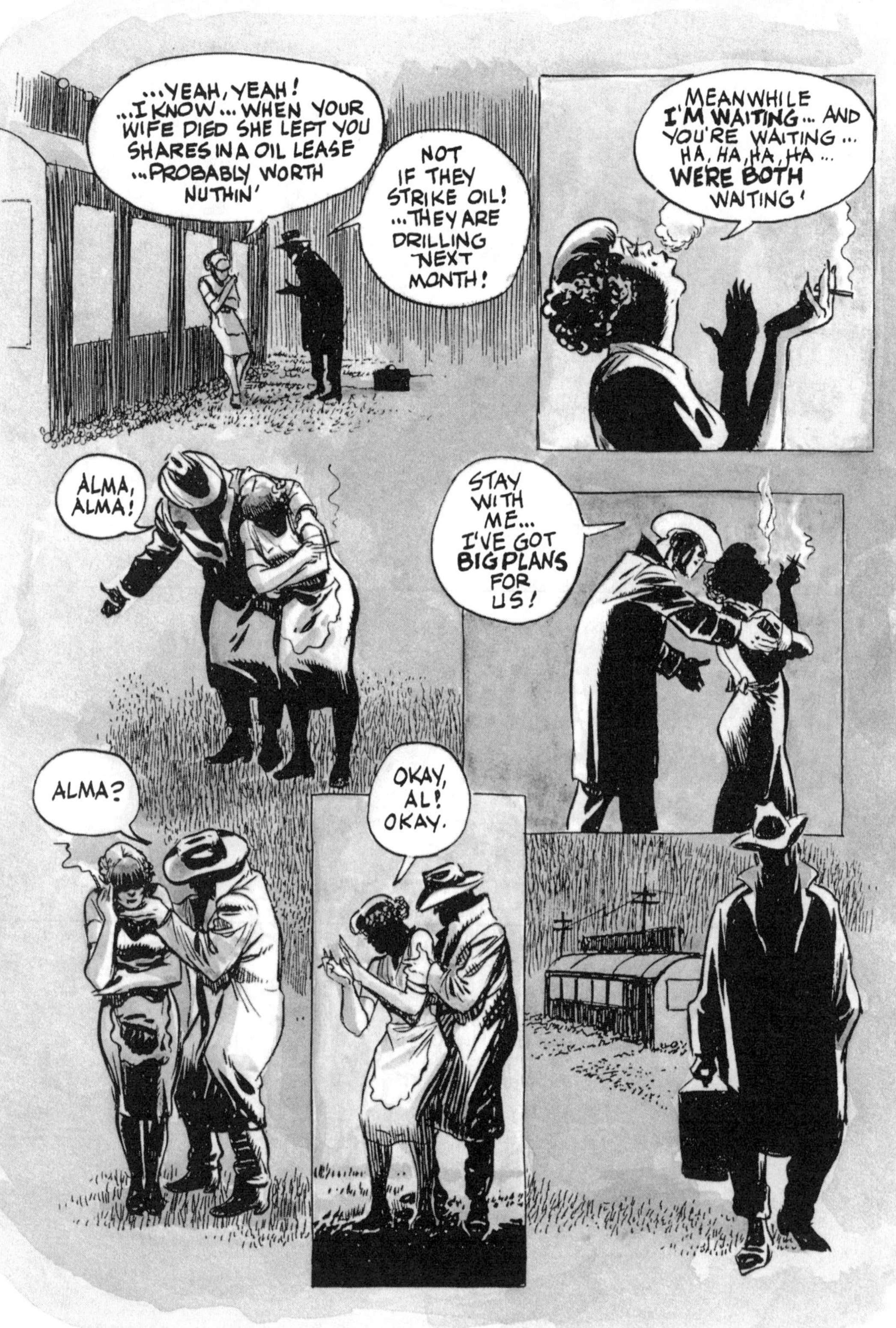
...YEAH, YEAH! ...I KNOW... WHEN YOUR WIFE DIED SHE LEFT YOU SHARES IN A OIL LEASE ...PROBABLY WORTH NUTHIN'
NOT IF THEY STRIKE OIL! ...THEY ARE DRILLING NEXT MONTH!
MEANWHILE I'M WAITING... AND YOU'RE WAITING... HA, HA, HA, HA... WERE BOTH WAITING!
ALMA, ALMA!
STAY WITH ME... I'VE GOT BIG PLANS FOR US!
ALMA?
OKAY, AL! OKAY.

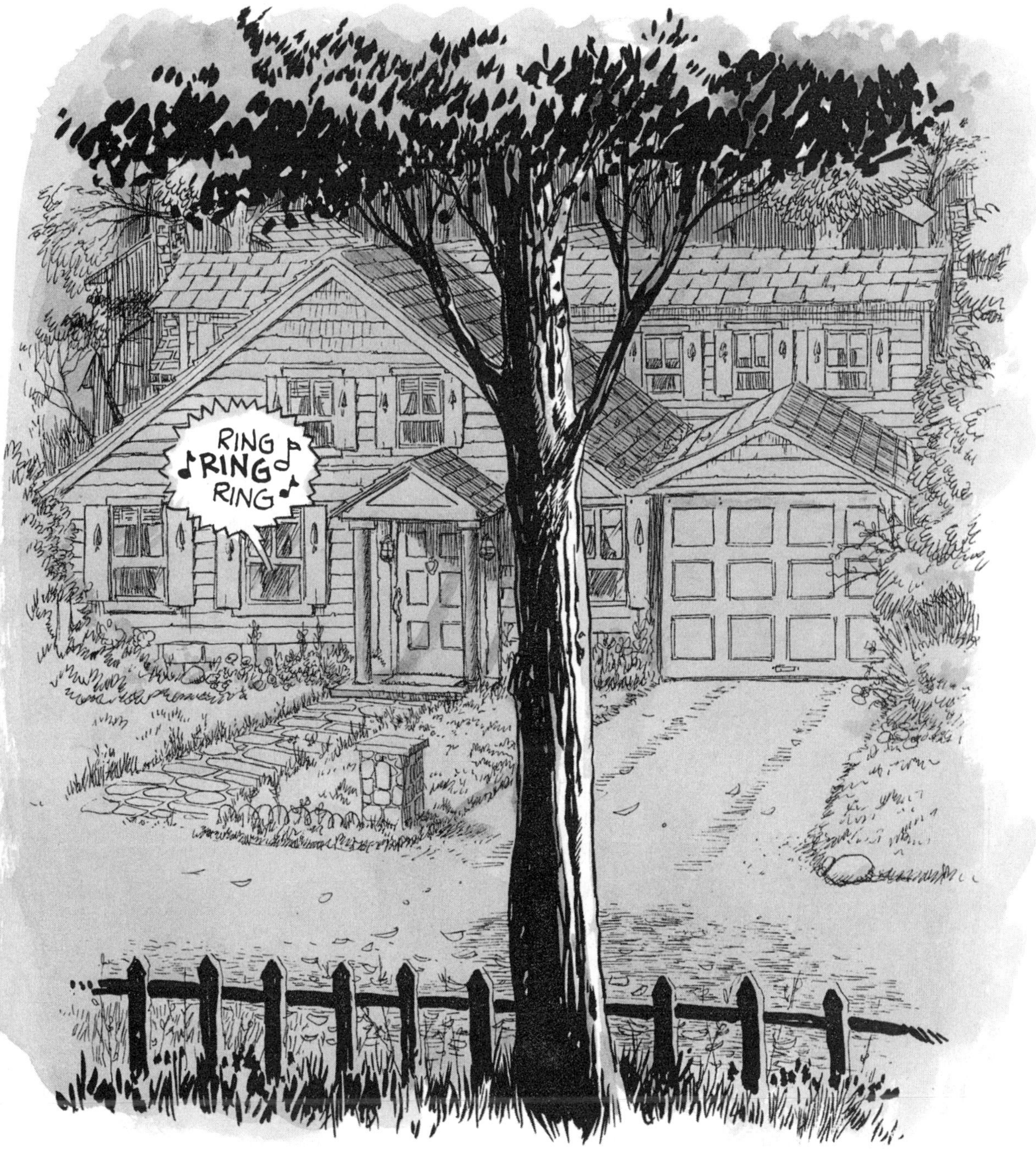
RING RING RING

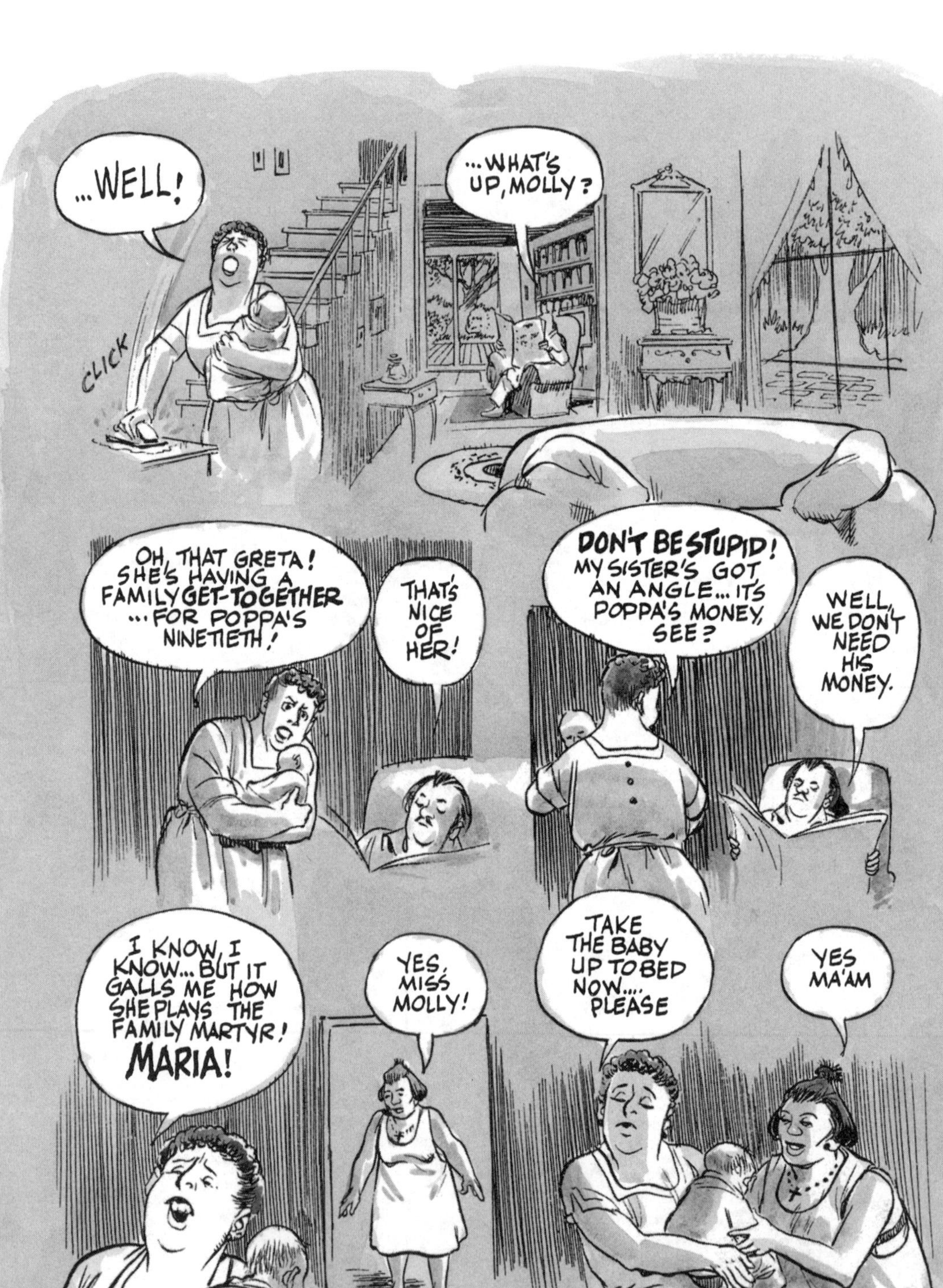
...WELL!
CLICK
...WHAT'S UP, MOLLY?
OH, THAT GRETA! SHE'S HAVING A FAMILY GET-TOGETHER ...FOR POPPA'S NINETIETH!
THAT'S NICE OF HER!
DON'T BE STUPID! MY SISTER'S GOT AN ANGLE... IT'S POPPA'S MONEY, SEE?
WELL, WE DON'T NEED HIS MONEY.
I KNOW, I KNOW... BUT IT GALLS ME HOW SHE PLAYS THE FAMILY MARTYR! MARIA!
YES, MISS MOLLY!
TAKE THE BABY UP TO BED NOW.... PLEASE
YES MA'AM

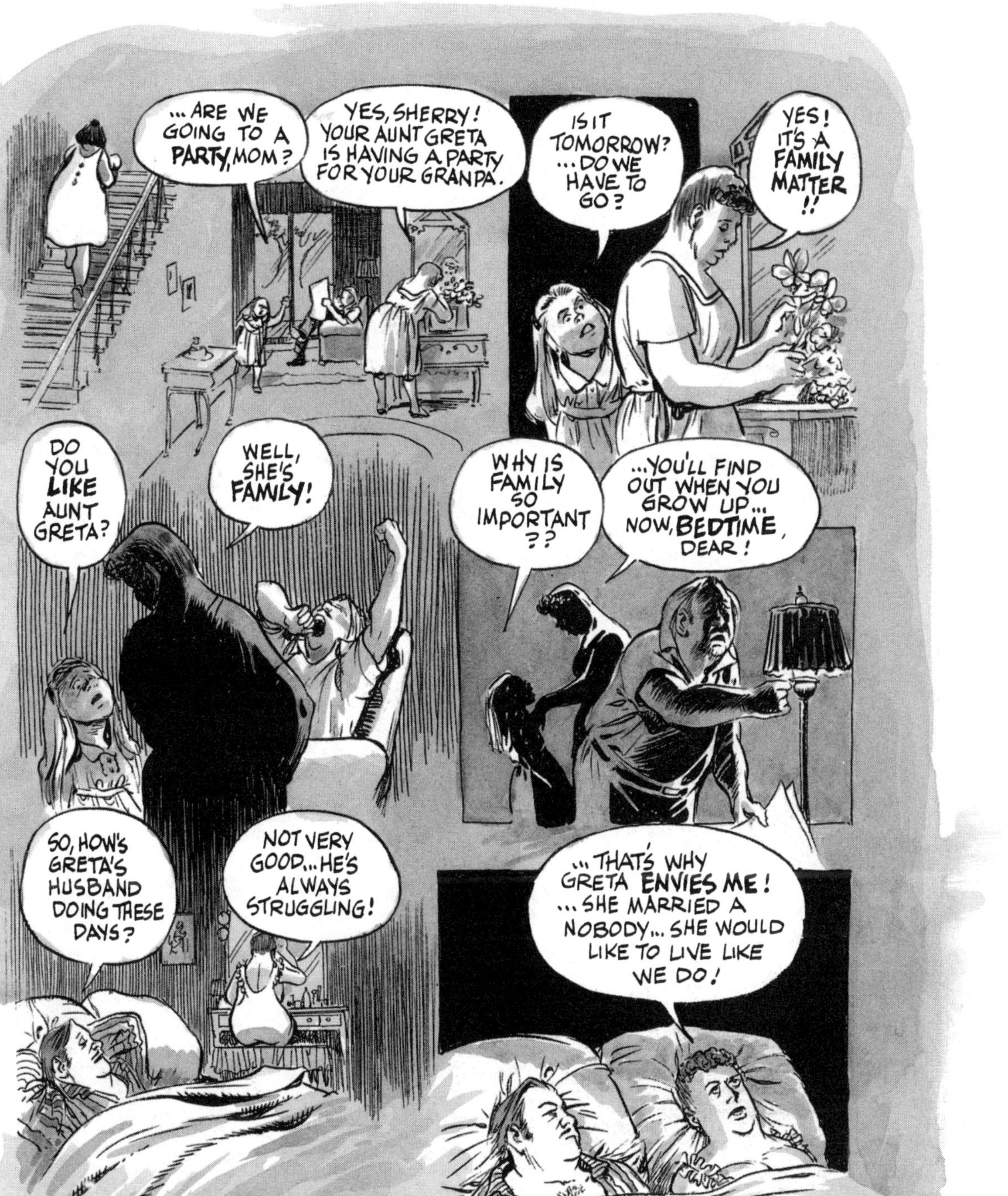
... ARE WE GOING TO A PARTY, MOM?
YES, SHERRY! YOUR AUNT GRETA IS HAVING A PARTY FOR YOUR GRANPA.
IS IT TOMORROW? ... DO WE HAVE TO GO?
YES! IT'S A FAMILY MATTER!!
DO YOU LIKE AUNT GRETA?
WELL, SHE'S FAMILY!
WHY IS FAMILY SO IMPORTANT??
...YOU'LL FIND OUT WHEN YOU GROW UP... NOW, BEDTIME, DEAR!
SO, HOW'S GRETA'S HUSBAND DOING THESE DAYS?
NOT VERY GOOD...HE'S ALWAYS STRUGGLING!
... THAT'S WHY GRETA ENVIES ME! ... SHE MARRIED A NOBODY... SHE WOULD LIKE TO LIVE LIKE WE DO!

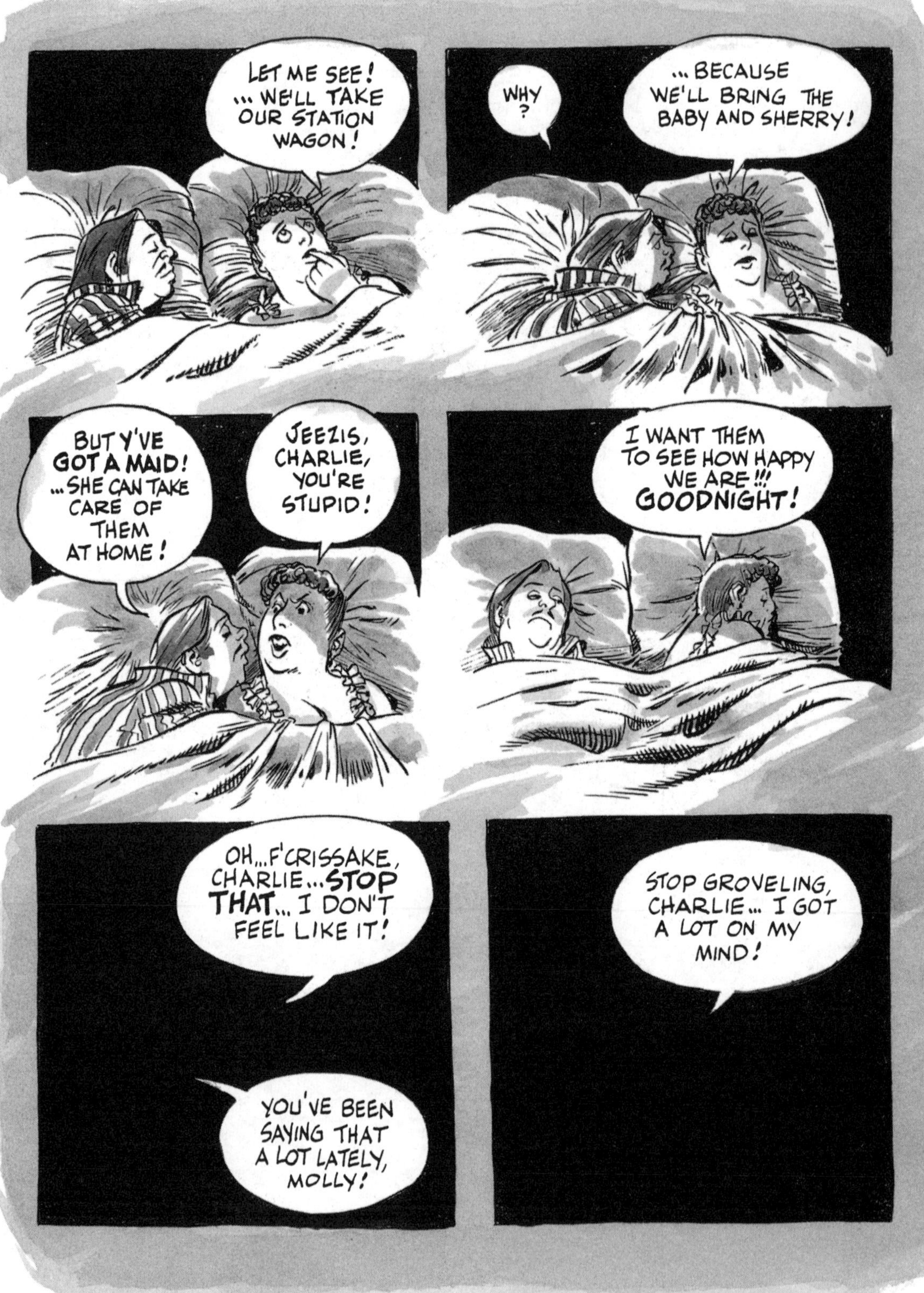
LET ME SEE! ... WE'LL TAKE OUR STATION WAGON!
WHY?
... BECAUSE WE'LL BRING THE BABY AND SHERRY!
BUT Y'VE GOT A MAID! ... SHE CAN TAKE CARE OF THEM AT HOME!
JEEZIS, CHARLIE, YOU'RE STUPID!
I WANT THEM TO SEE HOW HAPPY WE ARE!!! GOODNIGHT!
OH... F'CRISSAKE, CHARLIE... STOP THAT... I DON'T FEEL LIKE IT!
YOU'VE BEEN SAYING THAT A LOT LATELY, MOLLY!
STOP GROVELING, CHARLIE... I GOT A LOT ON MY MIND!

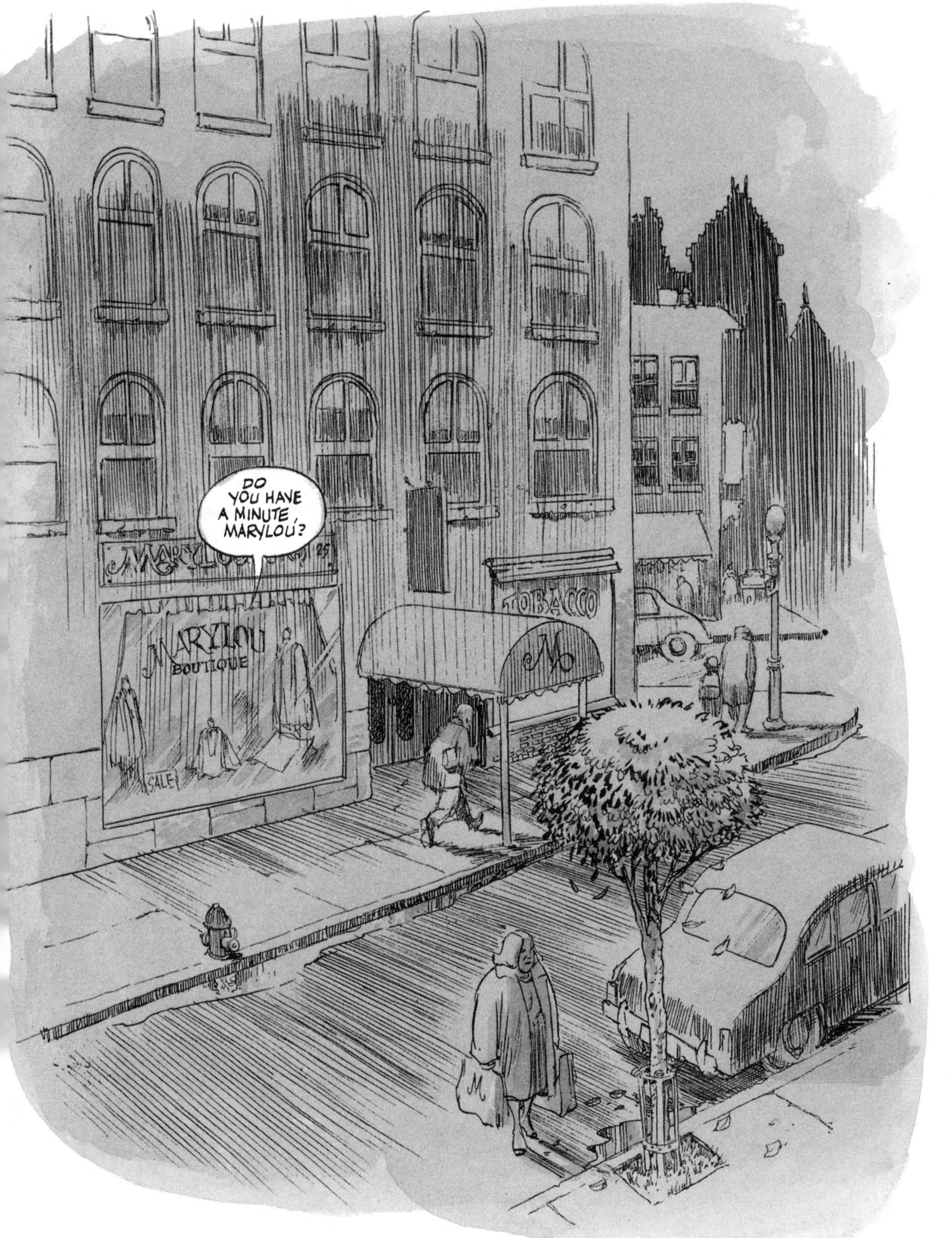
DO YOU HAVE A MINUTE, MARYLOU?
MARYLOU
MARYLOU BOUTIQUE
SALE
TOBACCO

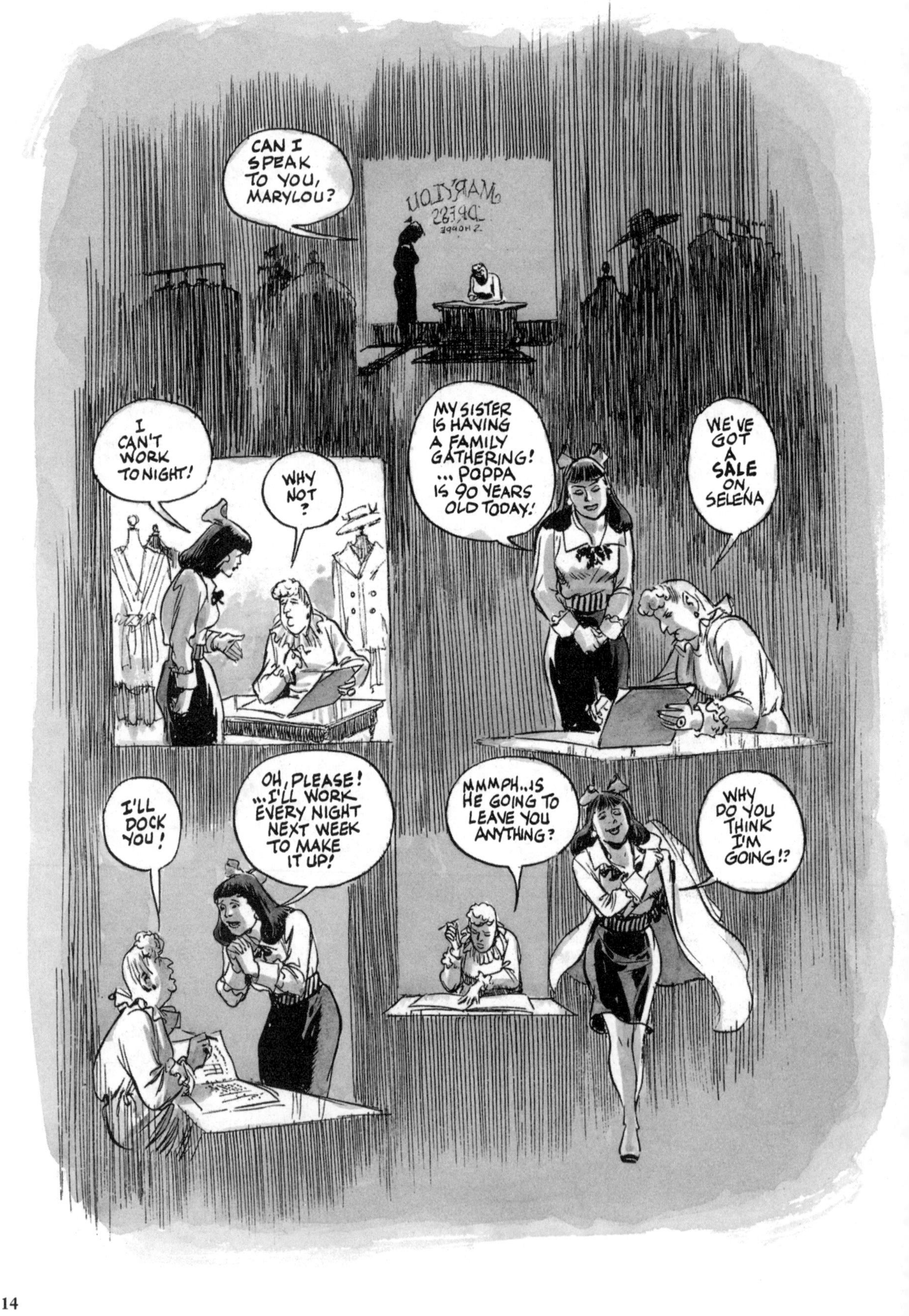
CAN I SPEAK TO YOU, MARYLOU?
I CAN'T WORK TONIGHT!
WHY NOT?
MY SISTER IS HAVING A FAMILY GATHERING! ... POPPA IS 90 YEARS OLD TODAY!
WE'VE GOT A SALE ON SELENA
I'LL DOCK YOU!
OH, PLEASE! ..I'LL WORK EVERY NIGHT NEXT WEEK TO MAKE IT UP!
MMMPH..IS HE GOING TO LEAVE YOU ANYTHING?
WHY DO YOU THINK I'M GOING!?

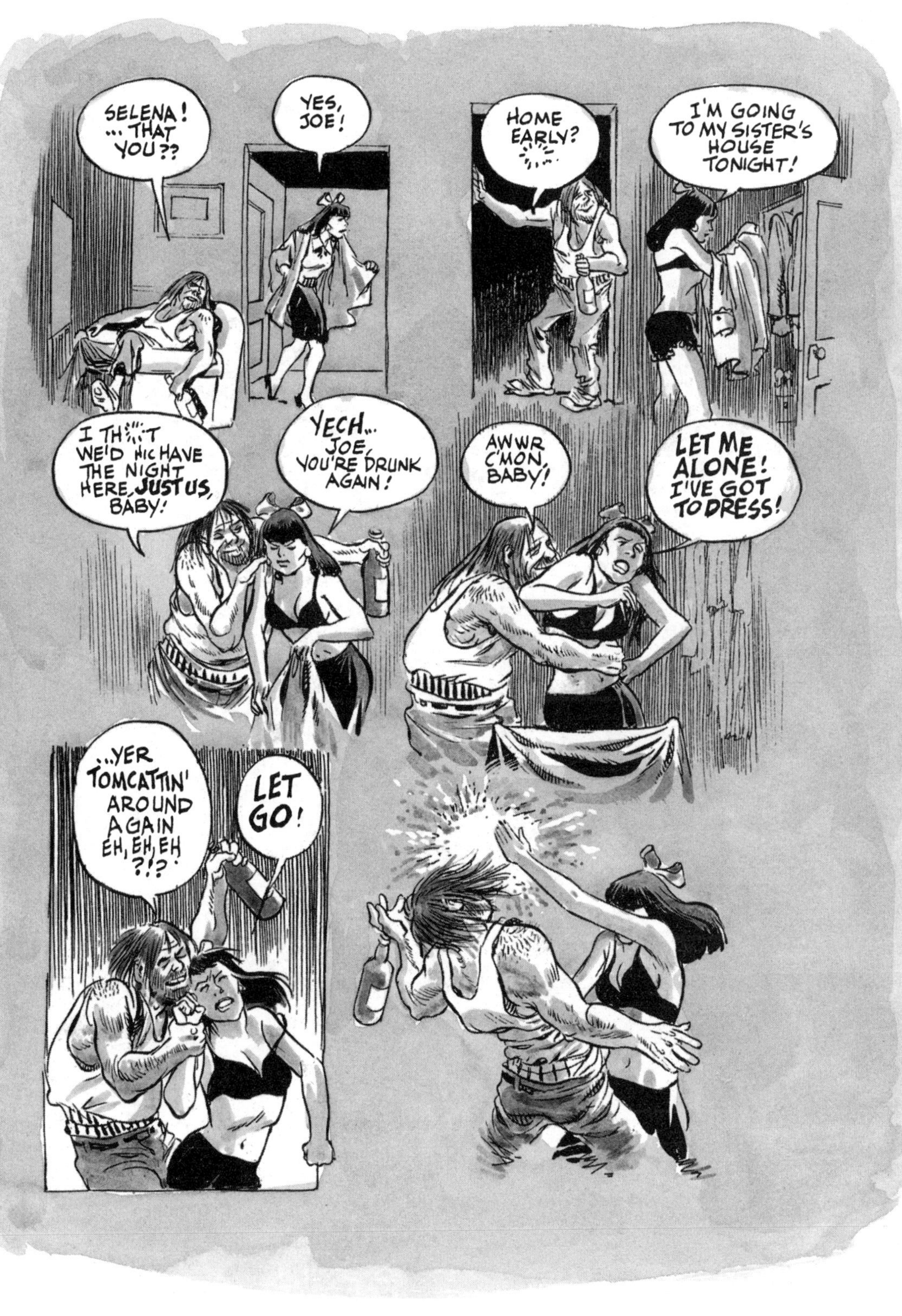
SELENA! ... THAT YOU??
YES, JOE!
HOME EARLY?
I'M GOING TO MY SISTER'S HOUSE TONIGHT!
I TH T WE'D HIC HAVE THE NIGHT HERE, JUST US, BABY!
YECH... JOE, YOU'RE DRUNK AGAIN!
AWWR C'MON, BABY!
LET ME ALONE! I'VE GOT TO DRESS!
...YER TOMCATTIN' AROUND AGAIN EH, EH, EH ?!?
LET GO!

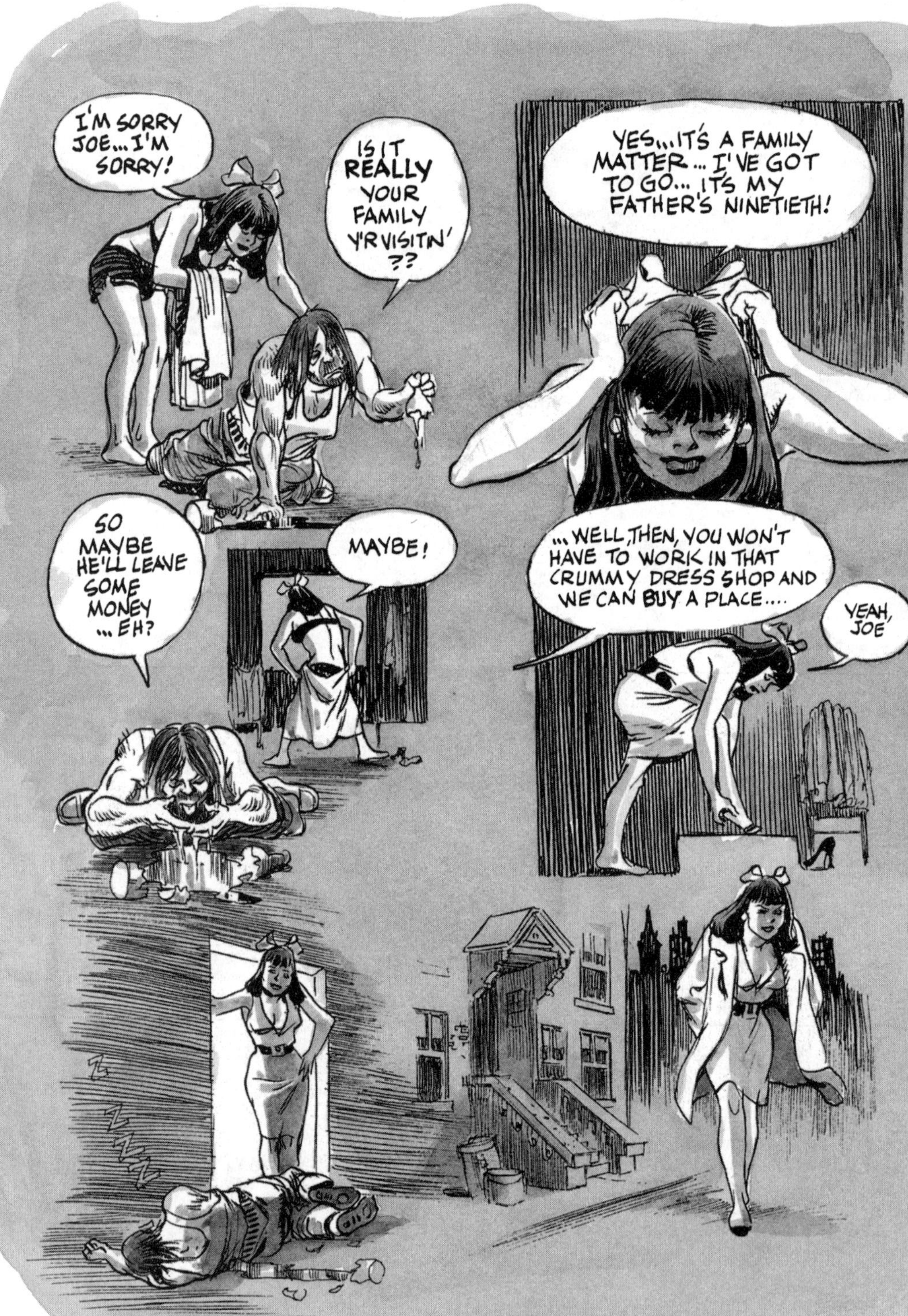
I'M SORRY JOE...I'M SORRY!
IS IT REALLY YOUR FAMILY Y'R VISITIN' ??
YES...IT'S A FAMILY MATTER... I'VE GOT TO GO... IT'S MY FATHER'S NINETIETH!
SO MAYBE HE'LL LEAVE SOME MONEY ...EH?
MAYBE!
...WELL, THEN, YOU WON'T HAVE TO WORK IN THAT CRUMMY DRESS SHOP AND WE CAN BUY A PLACE....
YEAH, JOE
Z
ZZZZ

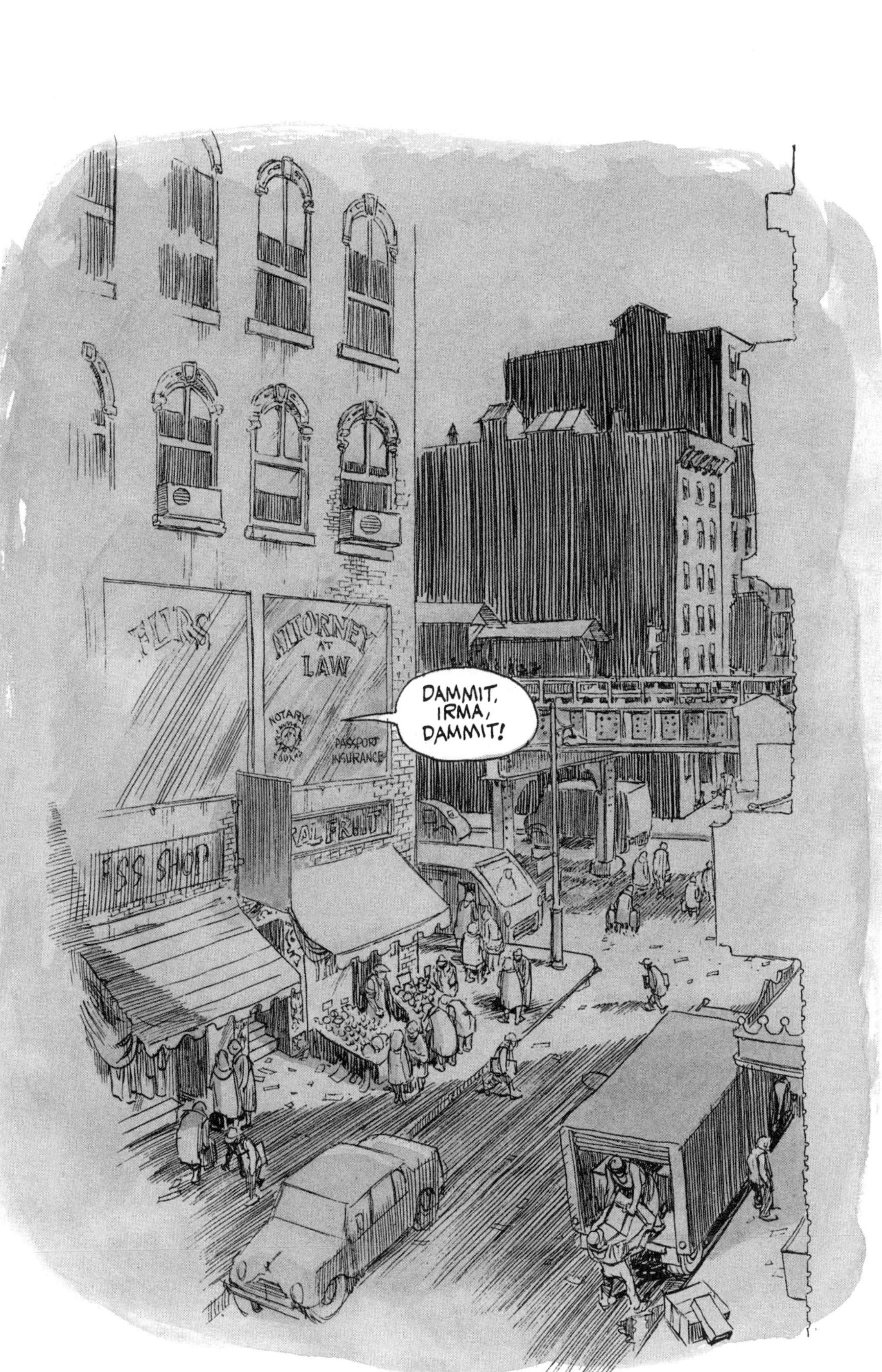
FURS
ATTORNEY
AT
LAW
NOTARY
PASSPORT
INSURANCE
DAMMIT, IRMA, DAMMIT!
RAL FRUIT
FISS SHOP

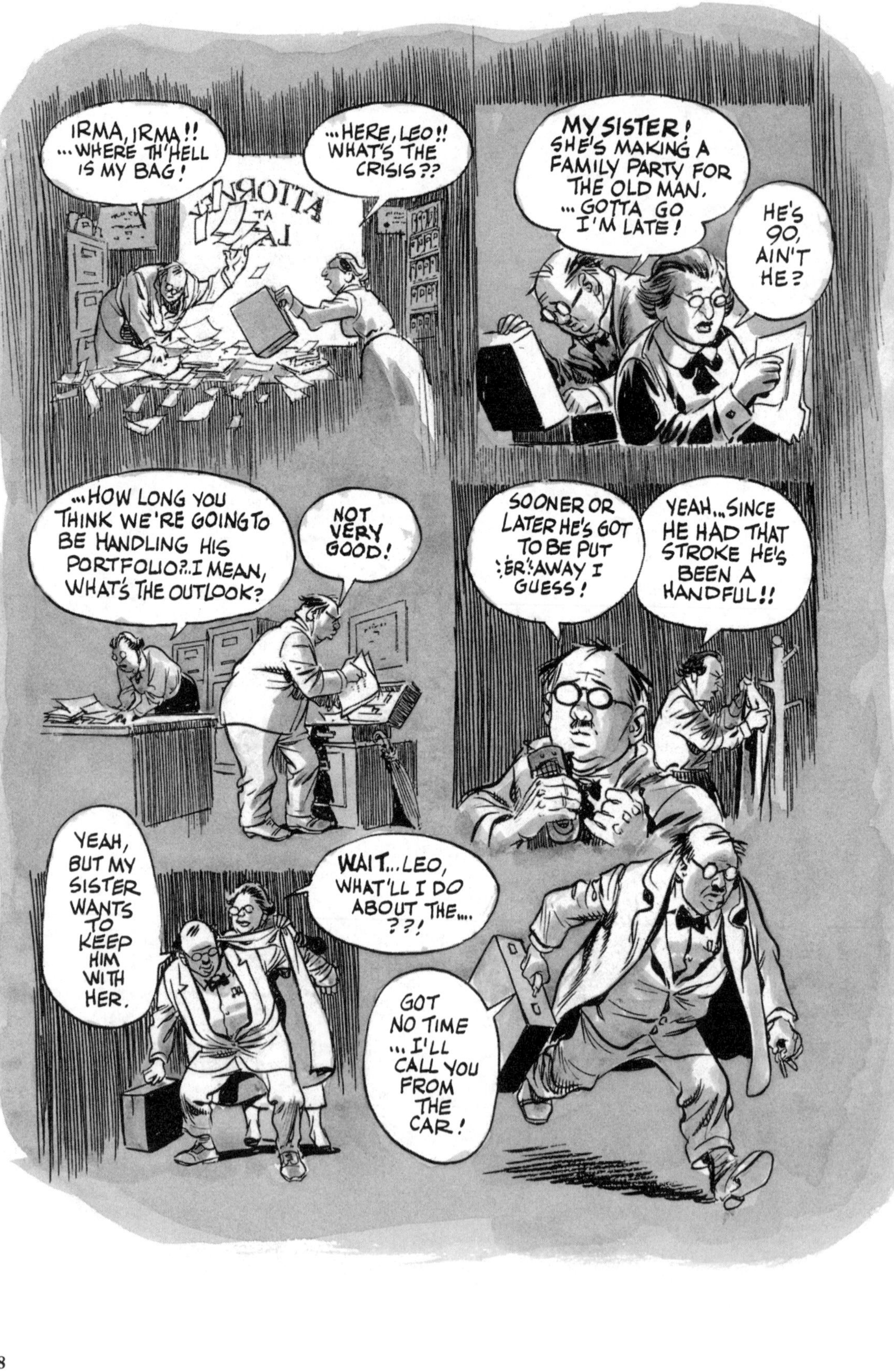
IRMA, IRMA!! ...WHERE TH'HELL IS MY BAG!
...HERE, LEO!! WHAT'S THE CRISIS??
MY SISTER! SHE'S MAKING A FAMILY PARTY FOR THE OLD MAN. ...GOTTA GO I'M LATE!
HE'S 90, AIN'T HE?
...HOW LONG YOU THINK WE'RE GOING TO BE HANDLING HIS PORTFOLIO?..I MEAN, WHAT'S THE OUTLOOK?
NOT VERY GOOD!
SOONER OR LATER HE'S GOT TO BE PUT ER AWAY I GUESS!
YEAH...SINCE HE HAD THAT STROKE HE'S BEEN A HANDFUL!!
YEAH, BUT MY SISTER WANTS TO KEEP HIM WITH HER.
WAIT...LEO, WHAT'LL I DO ABOUT THE.... ??!
GOT NO TIME ...I'LL CALL YOU FROM THE CAR!

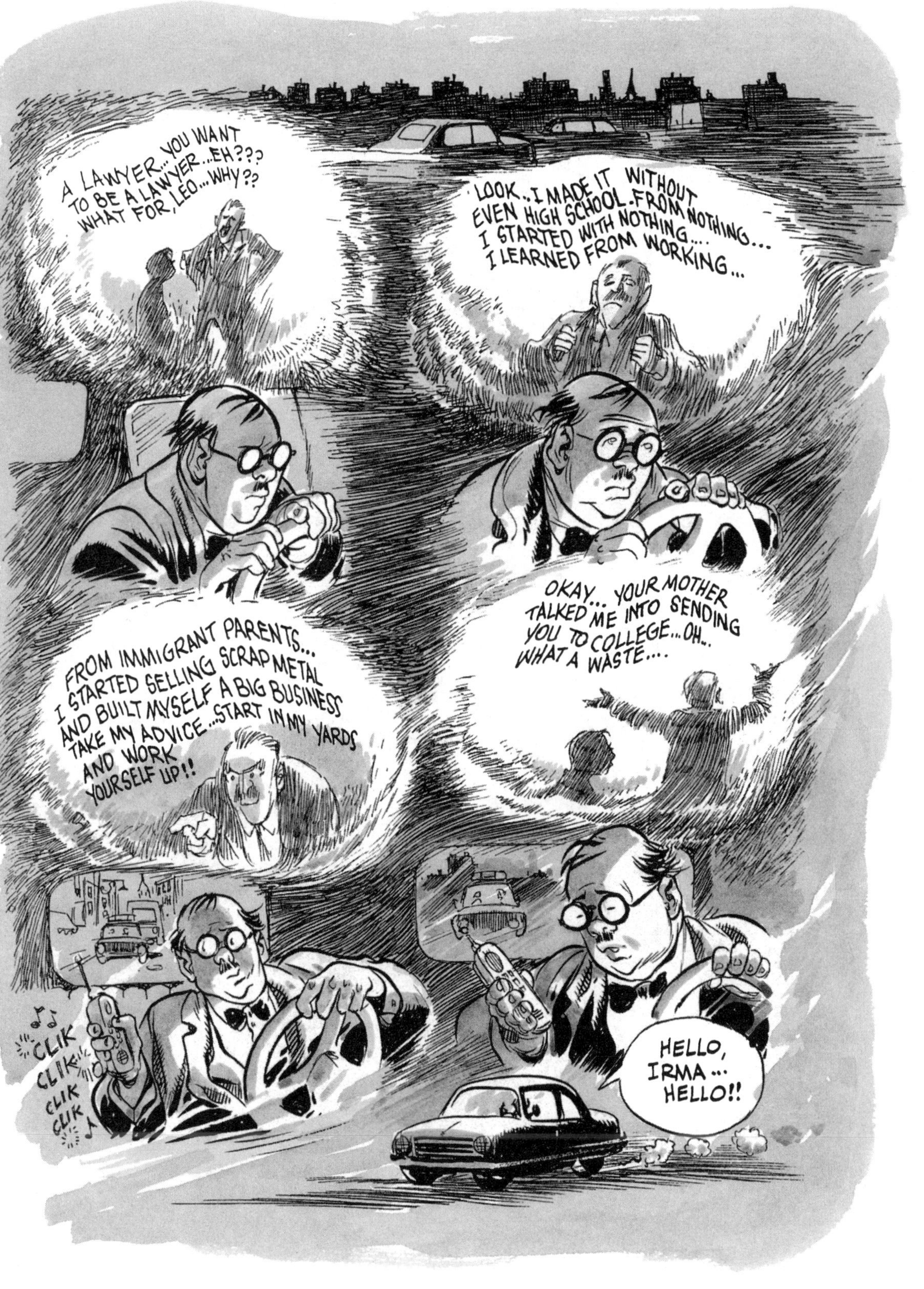
A LAWYER...YOU WANT TO BE A LAWYER...EH??? WHAT FOR, LEO...WHY??
LOOK..I MADE IT WITHOUT EVEN HIGH SCHOOL..FROM NOTHING... I STARTED WITH NOTHING.... I LEARNED FROM WORKING...
FROM IMMIGRANT PARENTS... I STARTED SELLING SCRAP METAL AND BUILT MYSELF A BIG BUSINESS TAKE MY ADVICE...START IN MY YARDS AND WORK YOURSELF UP!!
OKAY... YOUR MOTHER TALKED ME INTO SENDING YOU TO COLLEGE...OH.. WHAT A WASTE....
CLIK CLIK CLIK CLIK
HELLO, IRMA... HELLO!!

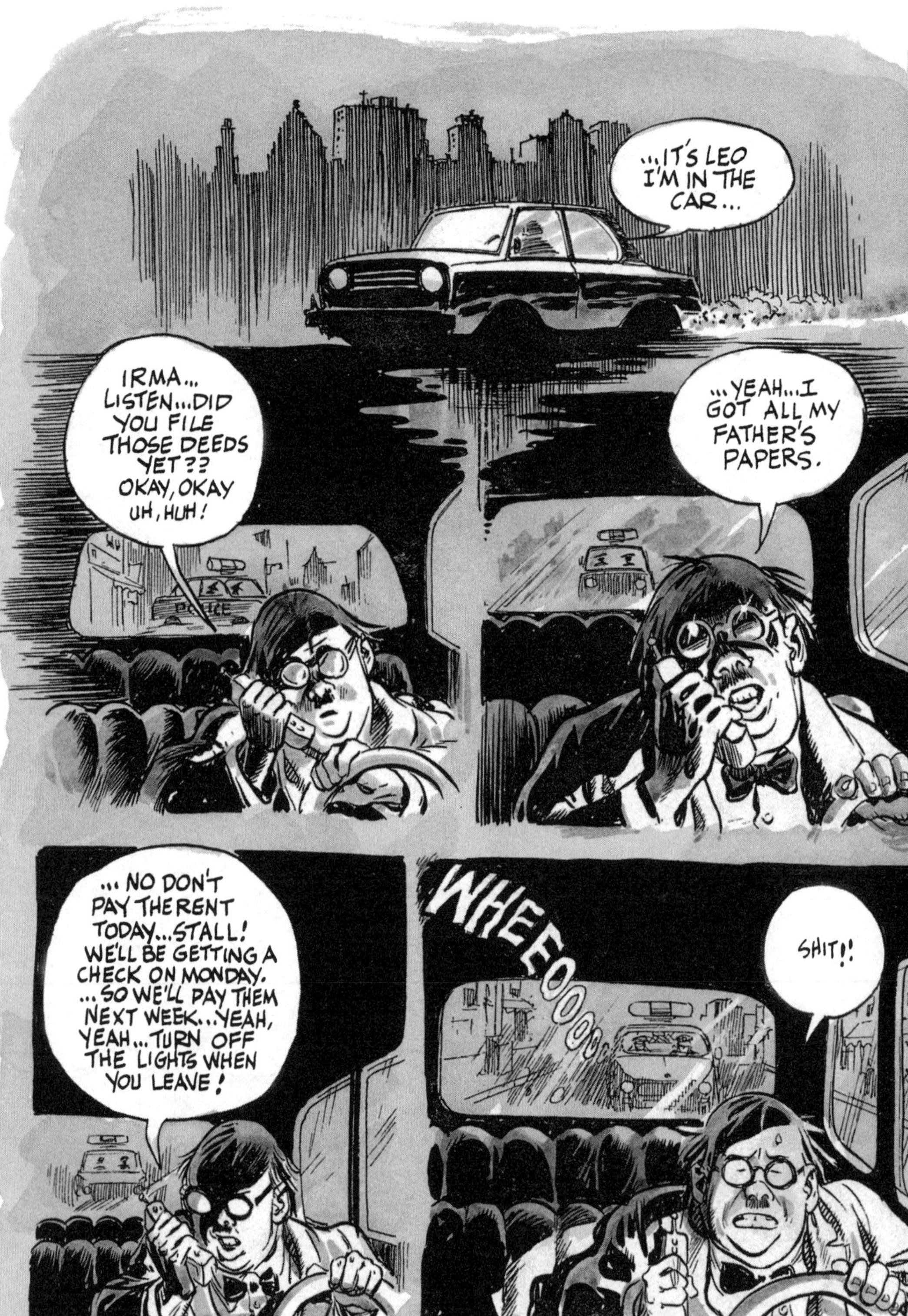
...IT'S LEO I'M IN THE CAR...
IRMA... LISTEN...DID YOU FILE THOSE DEEDS YET?? OKAY, OKAY UH, HUH!
...YEAH...I GOT ALL MY FATHER'S PAPERS.
... NO DON'T PAY THE RENT TODAY...STALL! WE'LL BE GETTING A CHECK ON MONDAY. ...SO WE'LL PAY THEM NEXT WEEK...YEAH, YEAH...TURN OFF THE LIGHTS WHEN YOU LEAVE!
WHEEOOOO
SHIT!!

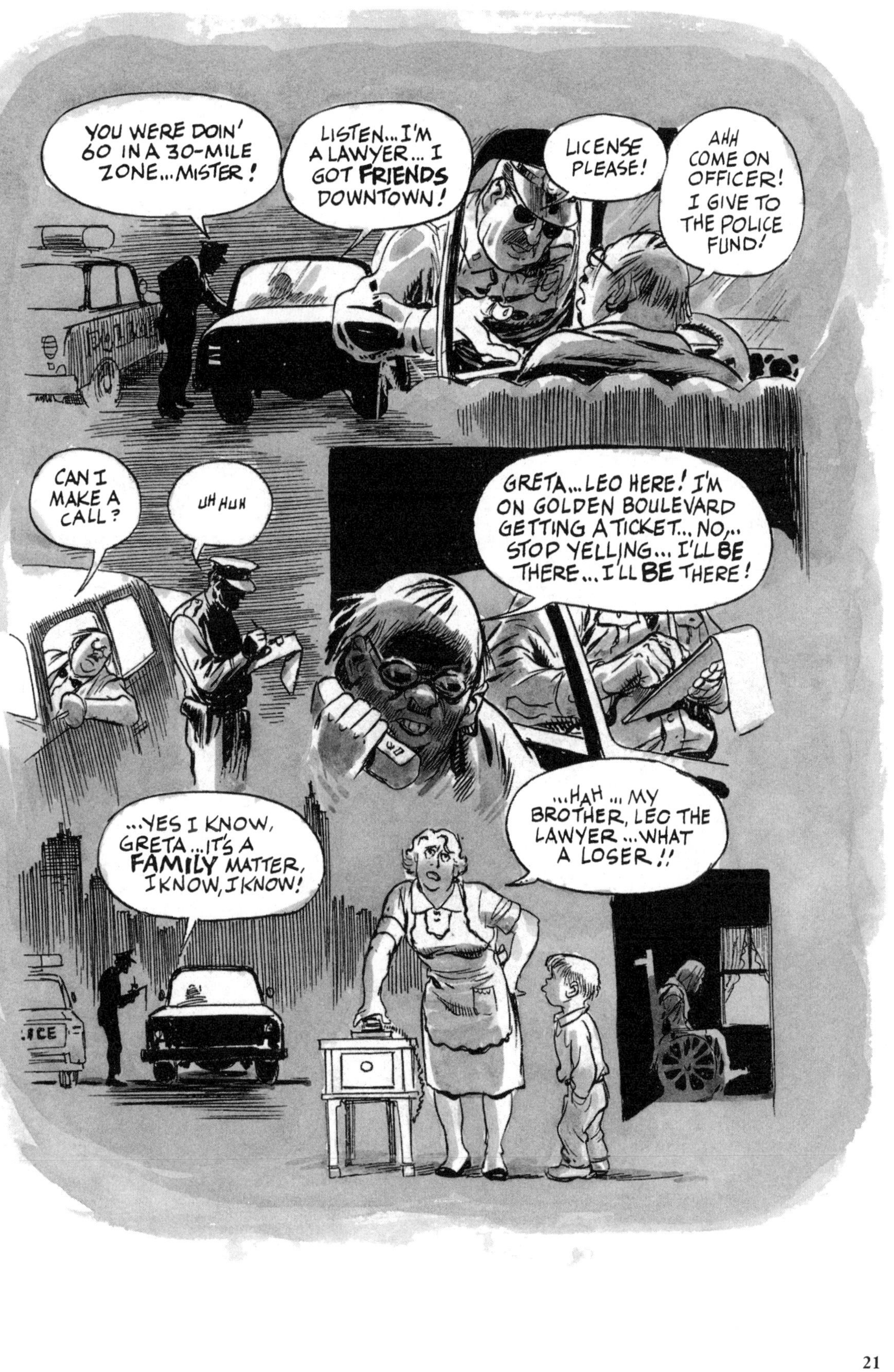
YOU WERE DOIN' 60 IN A 30-MILE ZONE...MISTER!
LISTEN...I'M A LAWYER... I GOT FRIENDS DOWNTOWN!
LICENSE PLEASE!
AHH COME ON OFFICER! I GIVE TO THE POLICE FUND!
CAN I MAKE A CALL?
UH HUH
GRETA...LEO HERE! I'M ON GOLDEN BOULEVARD GETTING A TICKET... NO,.. STOP YELLING... I'LL BE THERE... I'LL BE THERE!
...YES I KNOW, GRETA...IT'S A FAMILY MATTER, I KNOW, I KNOW!
...HAH ... MY BROTHER, LEO THE LAWYER ...WHAT A LOSER!!

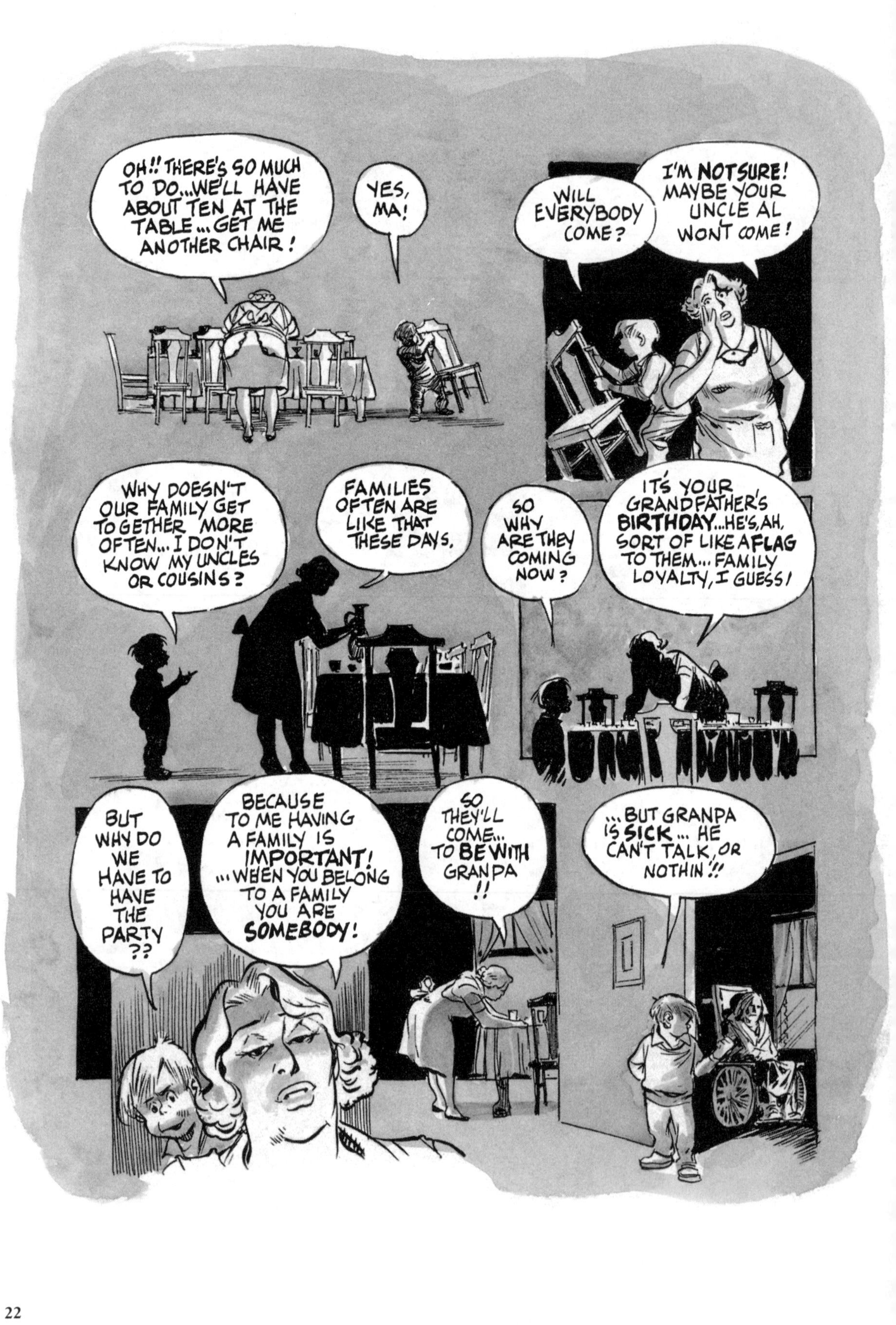
OH!! THERE'S SO MUCH TO DO...WE'LL HAVE ABOUT TEN AT THE TABLE...GET ME ANOTHER CHAIR!
YES, MA!
WILL EVERYBODY COME?
I'M NOT SURE! MAYBE YOUR UNCLE AL WON'T COME!
WHY DOESN'T OUR FAMILY GET TOGETHER MORE OFTEN...I DON'T KNOW MY UNCLES OR COUSINS?
FAMILIES OFTEN ARE LIKE THAT THESE DAYS.
SO WHY ARE THEY COMING NOW?
IT'S YOUR GRANDFATHER'S BIRTHDAY...HE'S, AH, SORT OF LIKE A FLAG TO THEM... FAMILY LOYALTY, I GUESS!
BUT WHY DO WE HAVE TO HAVE THE PARTY??
BECAUSE TO ME HAVING A FAMILY IS IMPORTANT! ...WHEN YOU BELONG TO A FAMILY YOU ARE SOMEBODY!
SO THEY'LL COME... TO BE WITH GRANPA!!
...BUT GRANPA IS SICK... HE CAN'T TALK, OR NOTHIN'!!

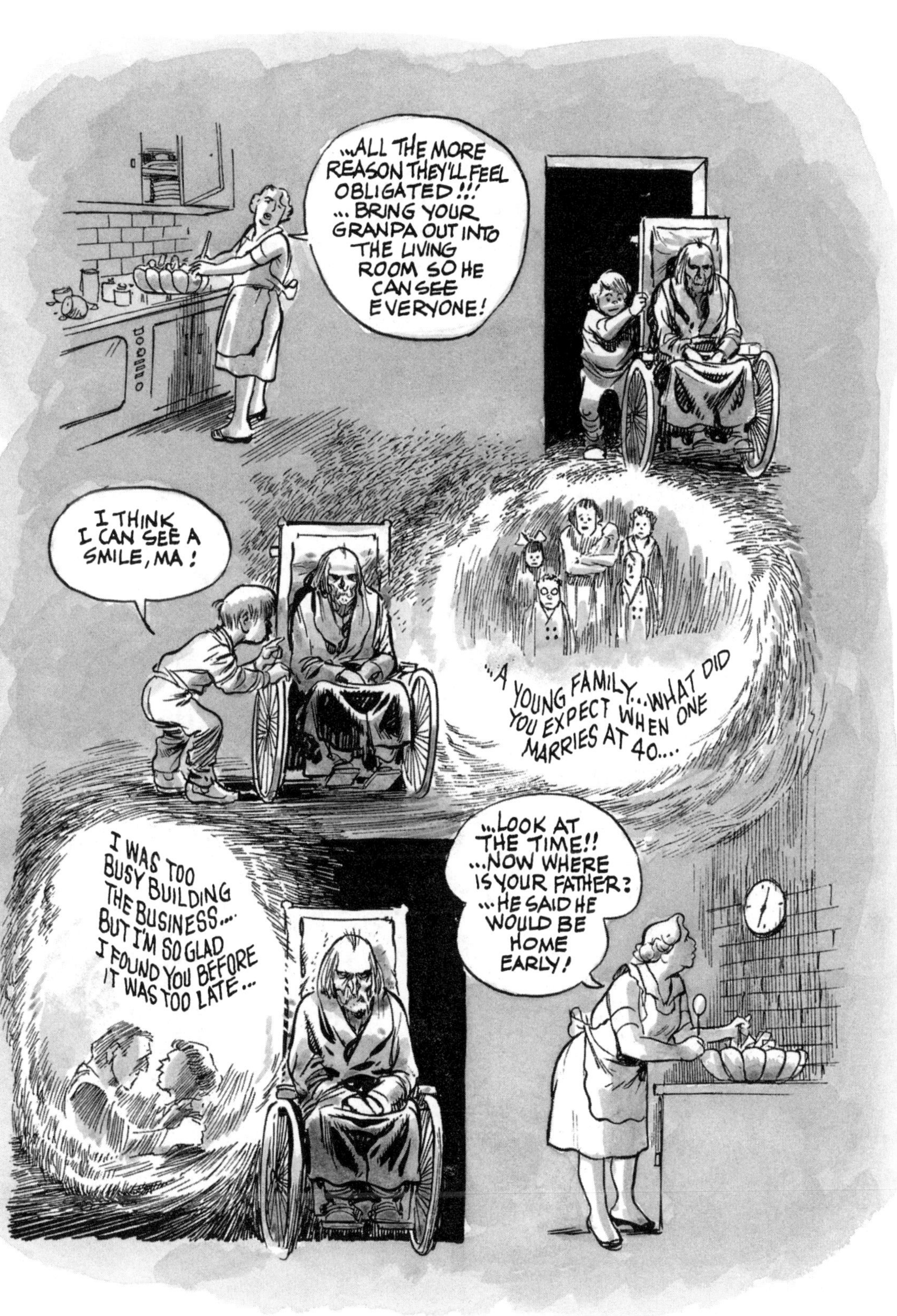
...ALL THE MORE REASON THEY'LL FEEL OBLIGATED!!! ... BRING YOUR GRANPA OUT INTO THE LIVING ROOM SO HE CAN SEE EVERYONE!
I THINK I CAN SEE A SMILE, MA!
...A YOUNG FAMILY...WHAT DID YOU EXPECT WHEN ONE MARRIES AT 40....
I WAS TOO BUSY BUILDING THE BUSINESS.... BUT I'M SO GLAD I FOUND YOU BEFORE IT WAS TOO LATE...
...LOOK AT THE TIME!! ...NOW WHERE IS YOUR FATHER? ...HE SAID HE WOULD BE HOME EARLY!

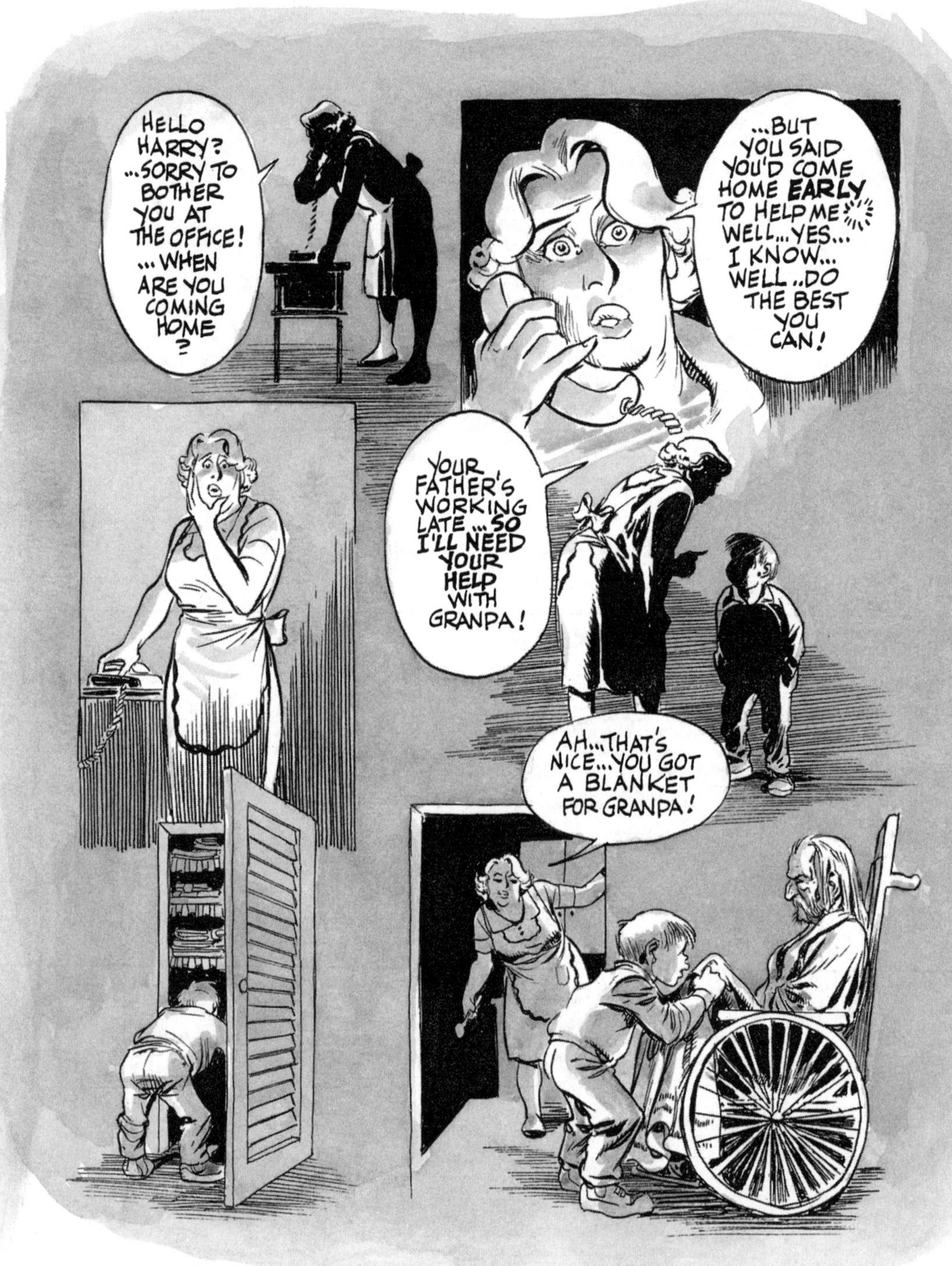
HELLO HARRY? ...SORRY TO BOTHER YOU AT THE OFFICE! ...WHEN ARE YOU COMING HOME?
...BUT YOU SAID YOU'D COME HOME EARLY TO HELP ME! WELL...YES... I KNOW... WELL..DO THE BEST YOU CAN!
YOUR FATHER'S WORKING LATE...SO I'LL NEED YOUR HELP WITH GRANPA!
AH...THAT'S NICE...YOU GOT A BLANKET FOR GRANPA!

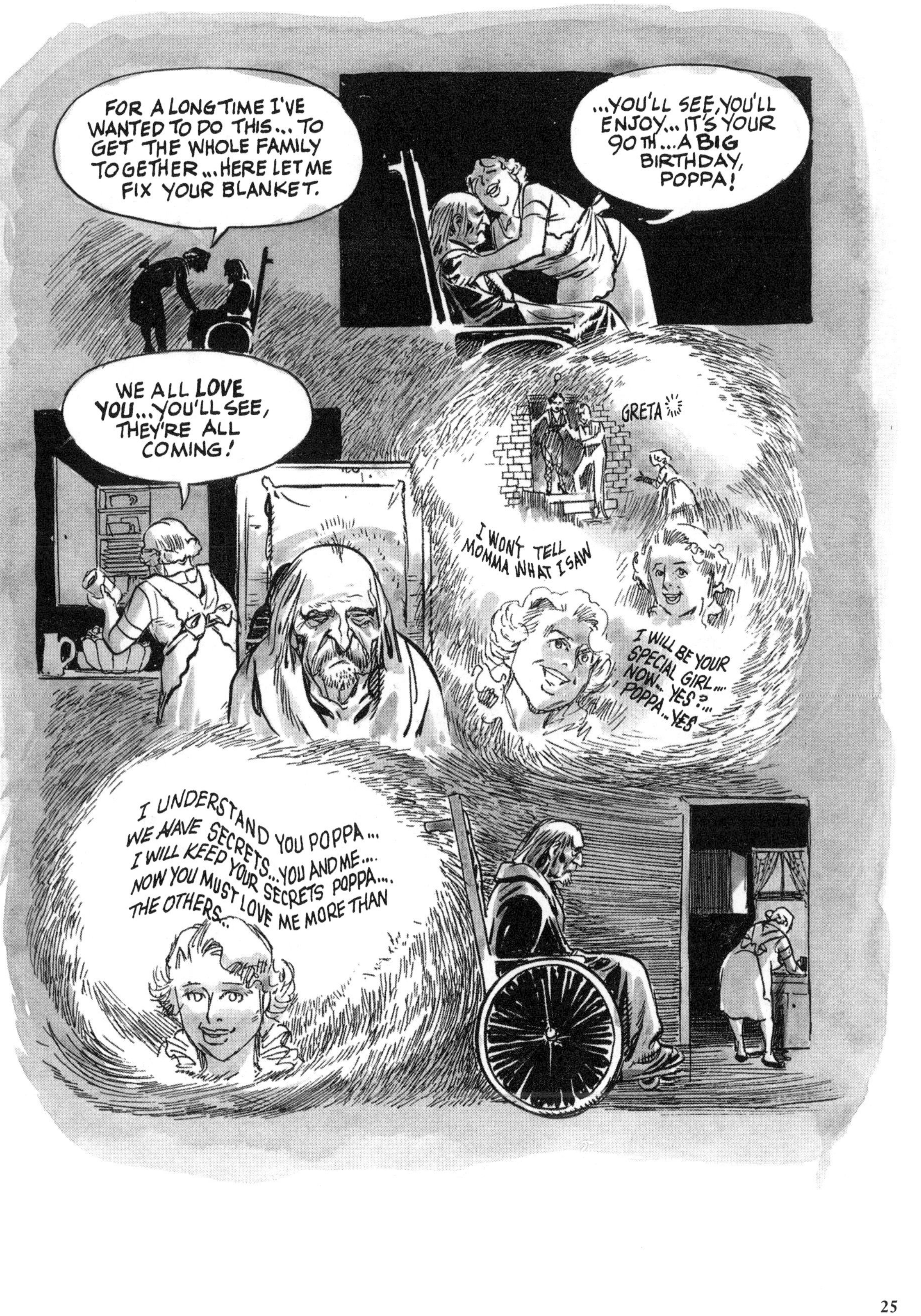
FOR A LONG TIME I'VE WANTED TO DO THIS... TO GET THE WHOLE FAMILY TOGETHER... HERE LET ME FIX YOUR BLANKET.
...YOU'LL SEE, YOU'LL ENJOY... IT'S YOUR 90TH... A BIG BIRTHDAY, POPPA!
WE ALL LOVE YOU... YOU'LL SEE, THEY'RE ALL COMING!
GRETA
I WON'T TELL MOMMA WHAT I SAW
I WILL BE YOUR SPECIAL GIRL.... NOW... YES?... POPPA... YES
I UNDERSTAND YOU POPPA...
WE HAVE SECRETS...YOU AND ME....
I WILL KEEP YOUR SECRETS POPPA....
NOW YOU MUST LOVE ME MORE THAN
THE OTHERS...

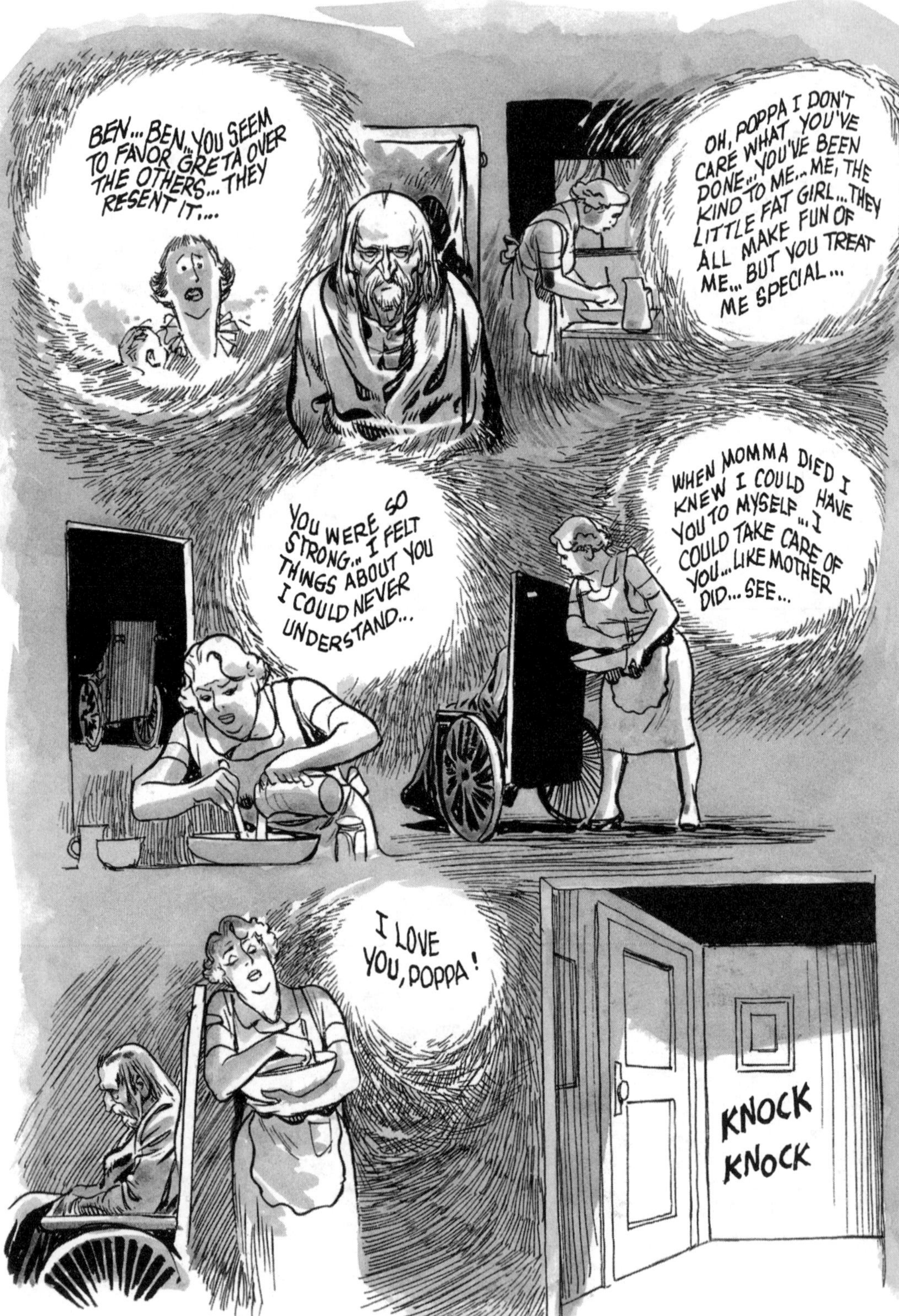
BEN... BEN... YOU SEEM TO FAVOR GRETA OVER THE OTHERS... THEY RESENT IT....
OH, POPPA I DON'T CARE WHAT YOU'VE DONE... YOU'VE BEEN KIND TO ME... ME, THE LITTLE FAT GIRL... THEY ALL MAKE FUN OF ME... BUT YOU TREAT ME SPECIAL...
YOU WERE SO STRONG... I FELT THINGS ABOUT YOU I COULD NEVER UNDERSTAND...
WHEN MOMMA DIED I KNEW I COULD HAVE YOU TO MYSELF... I COULD TAKE CARE OF YOU... LIKE MOTHER DID... SEE...
I LOVE YOU, POPPA!
KNOCK KNOCK

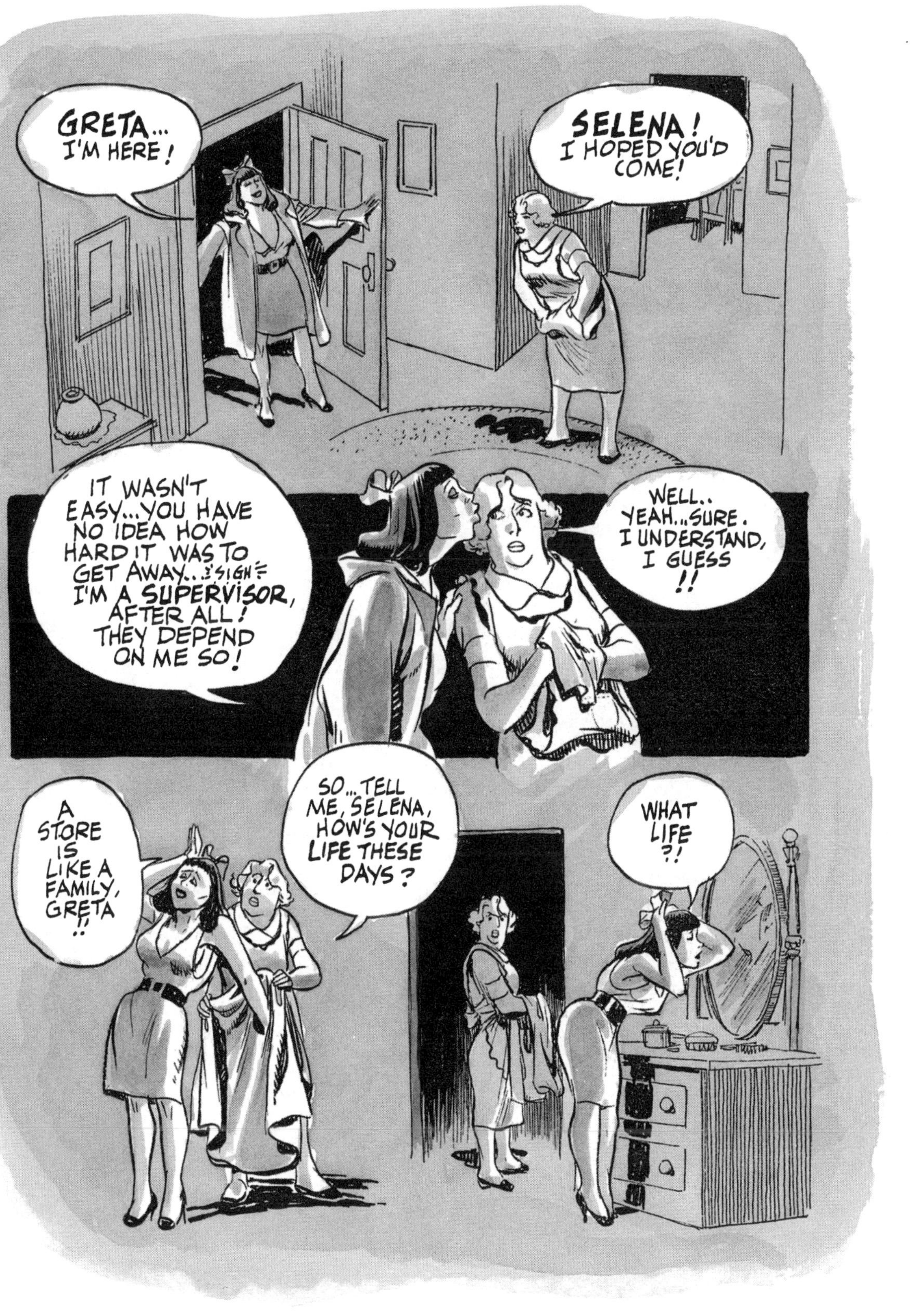
GRETA... I'M HERE!
SELENA! I HOPED YOU'D COME!
IT WASN'T EASY...YOU HAVE NO IDEA HOW HARD IT WAS TO GET AWAY... SIGH I'M A SUPERVISOR, AFTER ALL! THEY DEPEND ON ME SO!
WELL.. YEAH...SURE. I UNDERSTAND, I GUESS !!
A STORE IS LIKE A FAMILY, GRETA !!
SO...TELL ME, SELENA, HOW'S YOUR LIFE THESE DAYS?
WHAT LIFE ?!

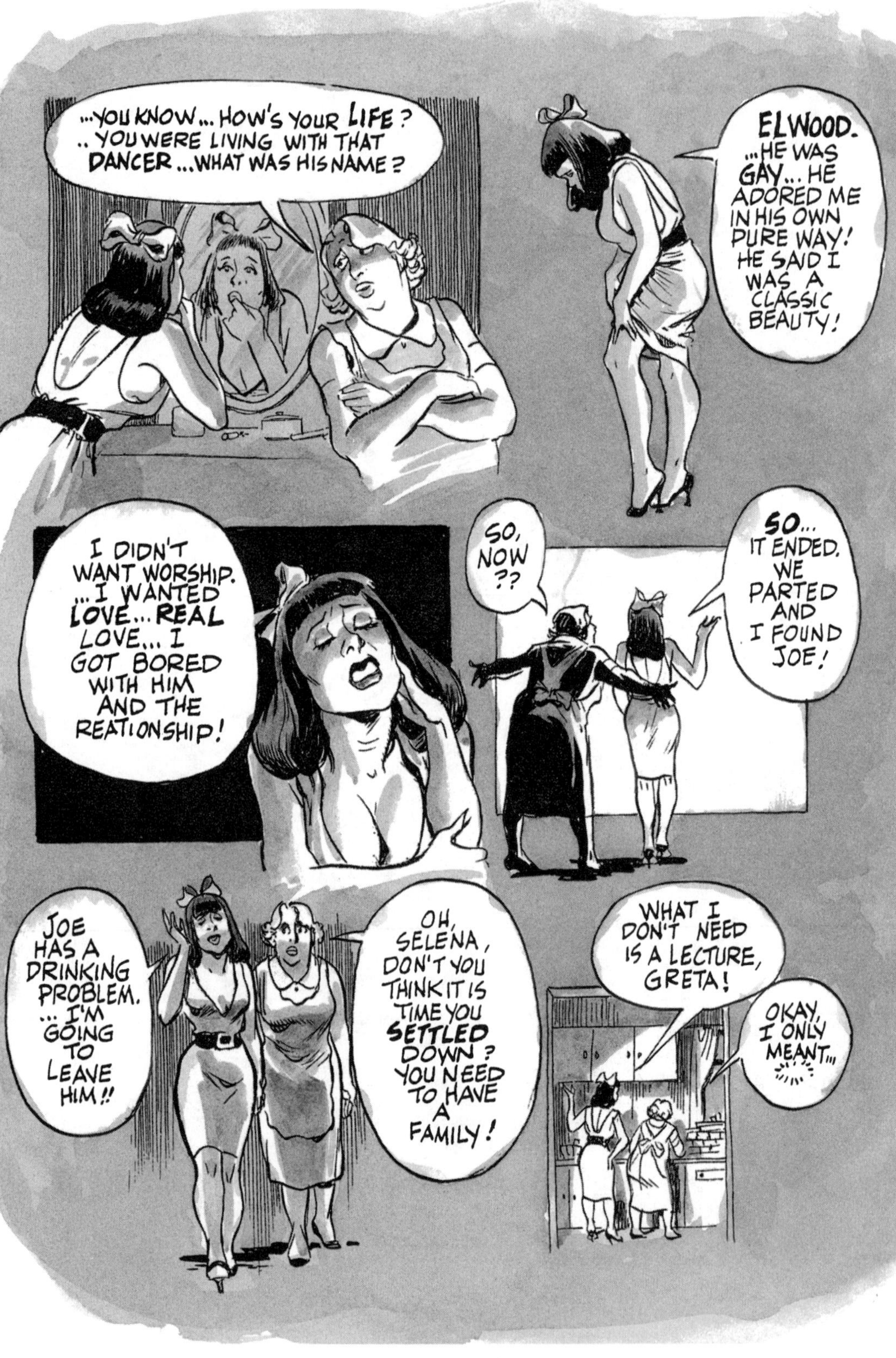
...YOU KNOW... HOW'S YOUR LIFE? .. YOU WERE LIVING WITH THAT DANCER ...WHAT WAS HIS NAME?
ELWOOD- ...HE WAS GAY... HE ADORED ME IN HIS OWN PURE WAY! HE SAID I WAS A CLASSIC BEAUTY!
I DIDN'T WANT WORSHIP. ...I WANTED LOVE... REAL LOVE... I GOT BORED WITH HIM AND THE REATIONSHIP!
SO, NOW ??
SO... IT ENDED. WE PARTED AND I FOUND JOE!
JOE HAS A DRINKING PROBLEM. ... I'M GOING TO LEAVE HIM!!
OH, SELENA, DON'T YOU THINK IT IS TIME YOU SETTLED DOWN? YOU NEED TO HAVE A FAMILY!
WHAT I DON'T NEED IS A LECTURE, GRETA!
OKAY, I ONLY MEANT...

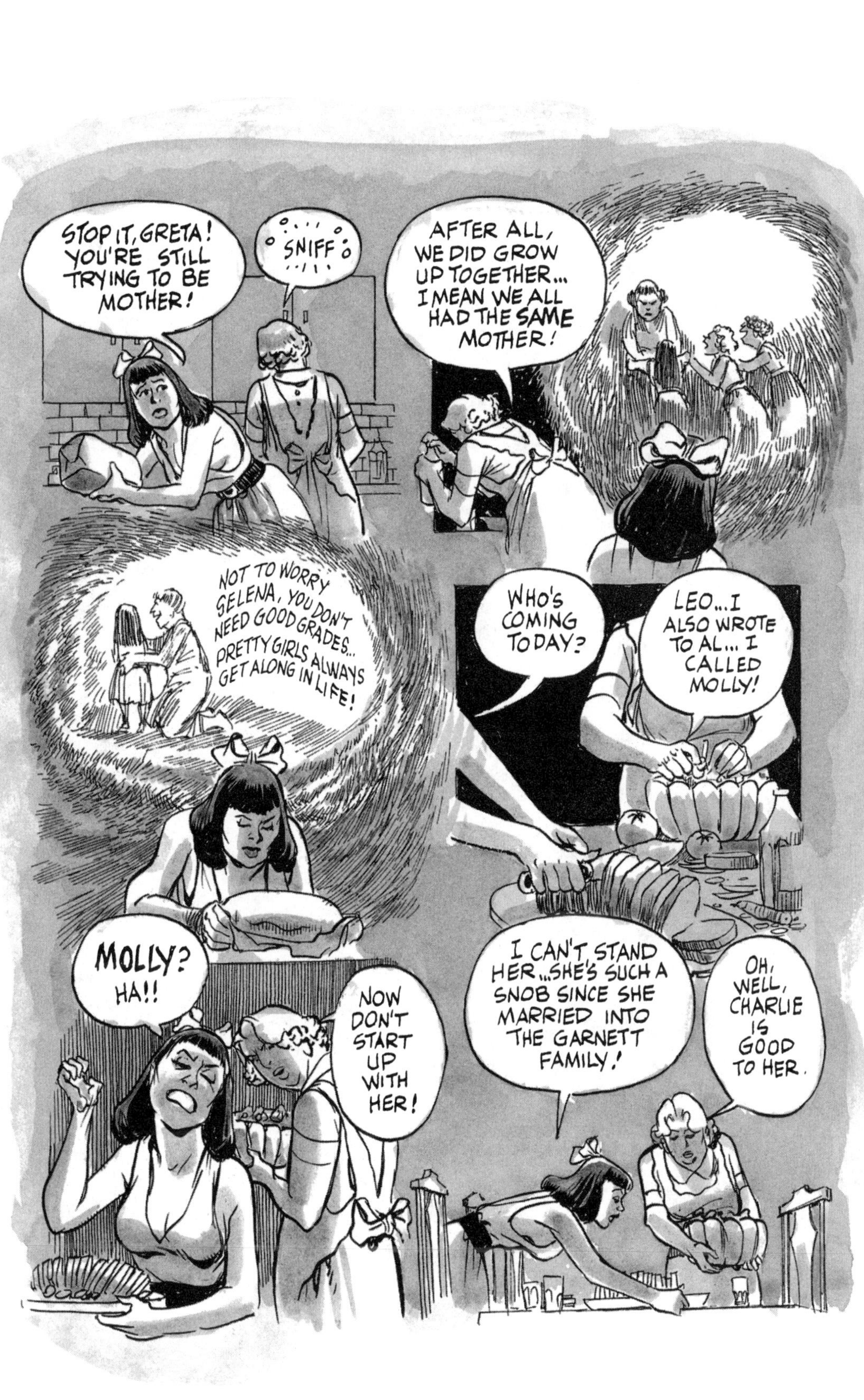
STOP IT, GRETA! YOU'RE STILL TRYING TO BE MOTHER!
SNIFF
AFTER ALL, WE DID GROW UP TOGETHER... I MEAN WE ALL HAD THE SAME MOTHER!
NOT TO WORRY SELENA, YOU DON'T NEED GOOD GRADES... PRETTY GIRLS ALWAYS GET ALONG IN LIFE!
WHO'S COMING TODAY?
LEO...I ALSO WROTE TO AL... I CALLED MOLLY!
MOLLY? HA!!
NOW DON'T START UP WITH HER!
I CAN'T STAND HER...SHE'S SUCH A SNOB SINCE SHE MARRIED INTO THE GARNETT FAMILY!
OH, WELL, CHARLIE IS GOOD TO HER.

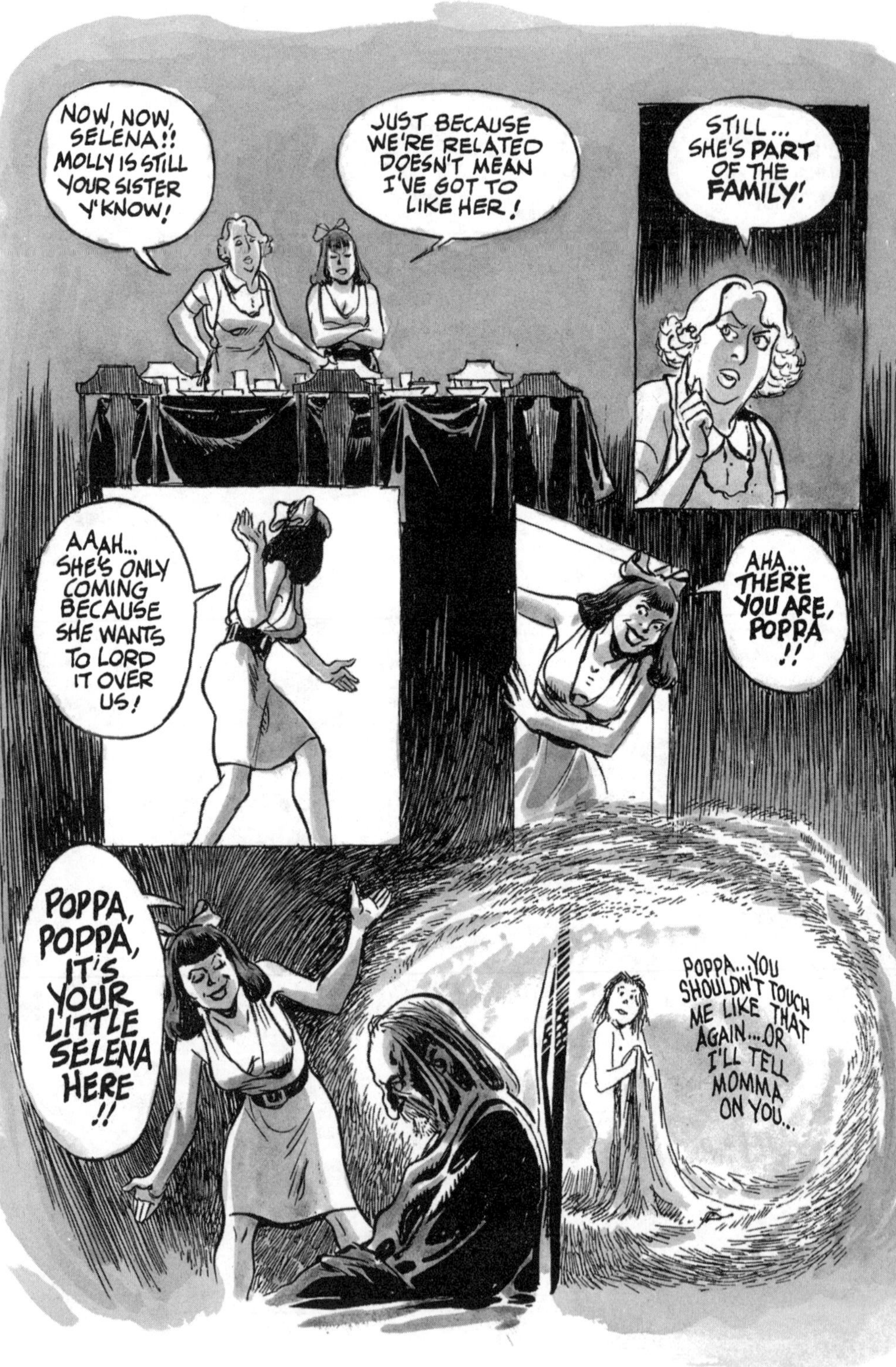
NOW, NOW, SELENA!! MOLLY IS STILL YOUR SISTER Y'KNOW!
JUST BECAUSE WE'RE RELATED DOESN'T MEAN I'VE GOT TO LIKE HER!
STILL... SHE'S PART OF THE FAMILY!
AAAH... SHE'S ONLY COMING BECAUSE SHE WANTS TO LORD IT OVER US!
AHA... THERE YOU ARE, POPPA!!
POPPA, POPPA, IT'S YOUR LITTLE SELENA HERE!!
POPPA... YOU SHOULDN'T TOUCH ME LIKE THAT AGAIN... OR I'LL TELL MOMMA ON YOU...

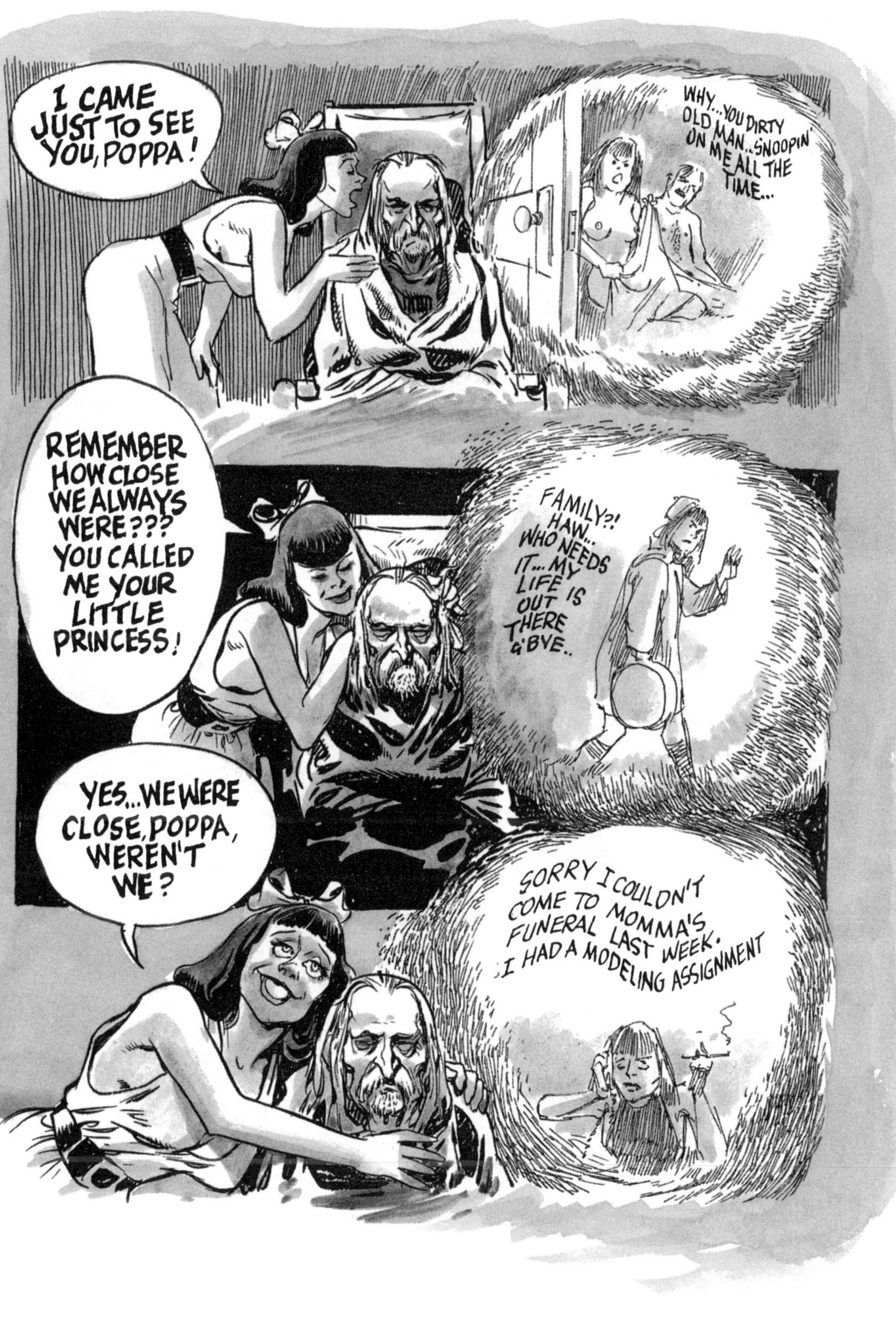
I CAME JUST TO SEE YOU, POPPA!
WHY...YOU DIRTY OLD MAN...SNOOPIN' ON ME ALL THE TIME...
REMEMBER HOW CLOSE WE ALWAYS WERE??? YOU CALLED ME YOUR LITTLE PRINCESS!
FAMILY?! HAW... WHO NEEDS IT...MY LIFE IS OUT THERE G'BYE..
YES...WE WERE CLOSE, POPPA, WEREN'T WE?
SORRY I COULDN'T COME TO MOMMA'S FUNERAL LAST WEEK. I HAD A MODELING ASSIGNMENT

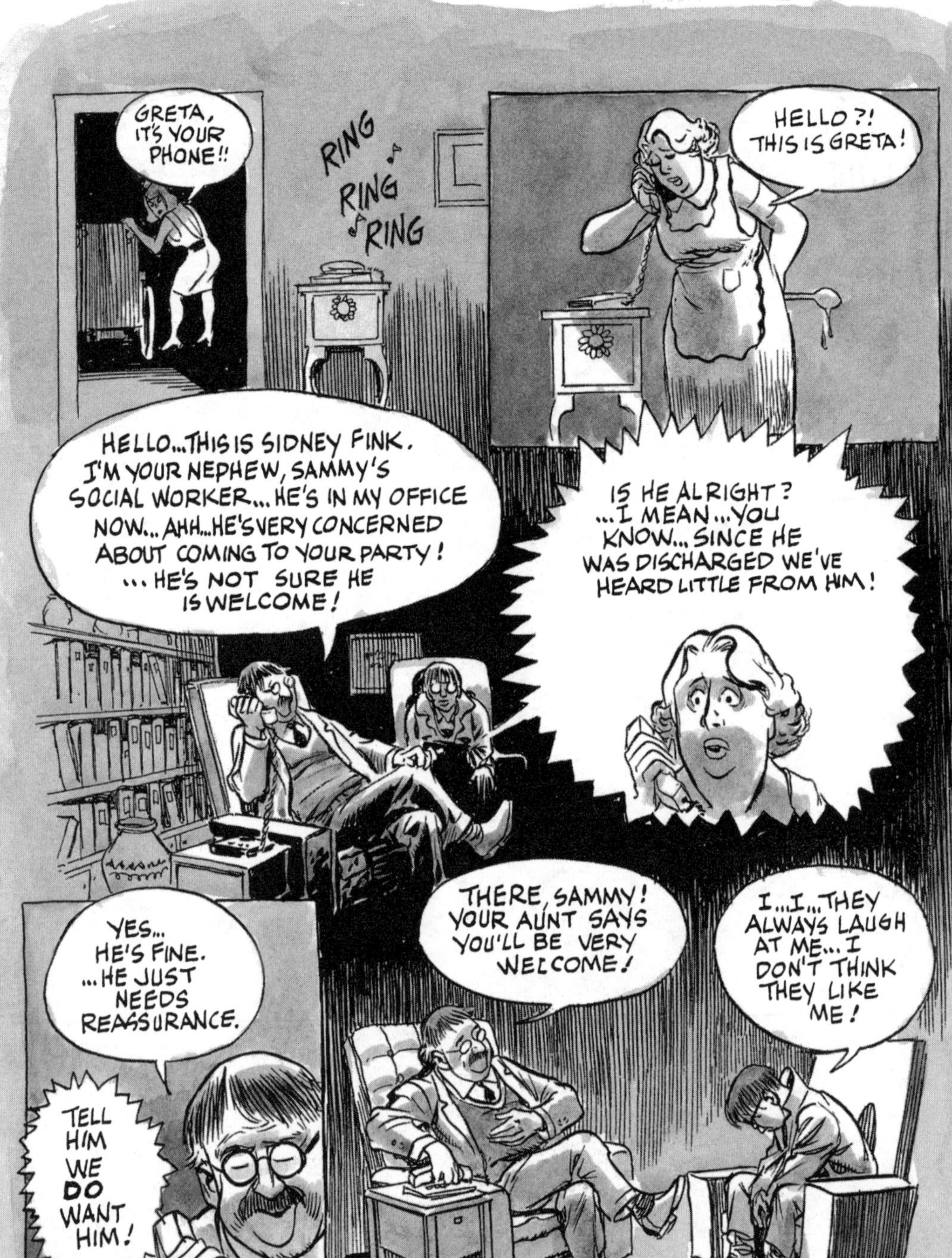
GRETA, IT'S YOUR PHONE!!
RING RING RING
HELLO?! THIS IS GRETA!
HELLO...THIS IS SIDNEY FINK. I'M YOUR NEPHEW, SAMMY'S SOCIAL WORKER... HE'S IN MY OFFICE NOW... AHH...HE'S VERY CONCERNED ABOUT COMING TO YOUR PARTY! ...HE'S NOT SURE HE IS WELCOME!
IS HE ALRIGHT? ...I MEAN...YOU KNOW... SINCE HE WAS DISCHARGED WE'VE HEARD LITTLE FROM HIM!
YES... HE'S FINE. ...HE JUST NEEDS REASSURANCE.
TELL HIM WE **DO** WANT HIM!
THERE, SAMMY! YOUR AUNT SAYS YOU'LL BE VERY WELCOME!
I...I...THEY ALWAYS LAUGH AT ME...I DON'T THINK THEY LIKE ME!

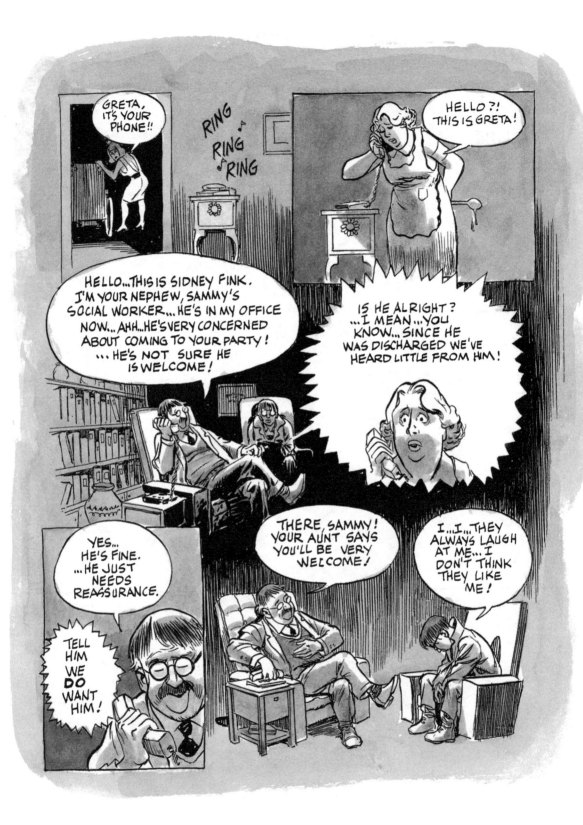

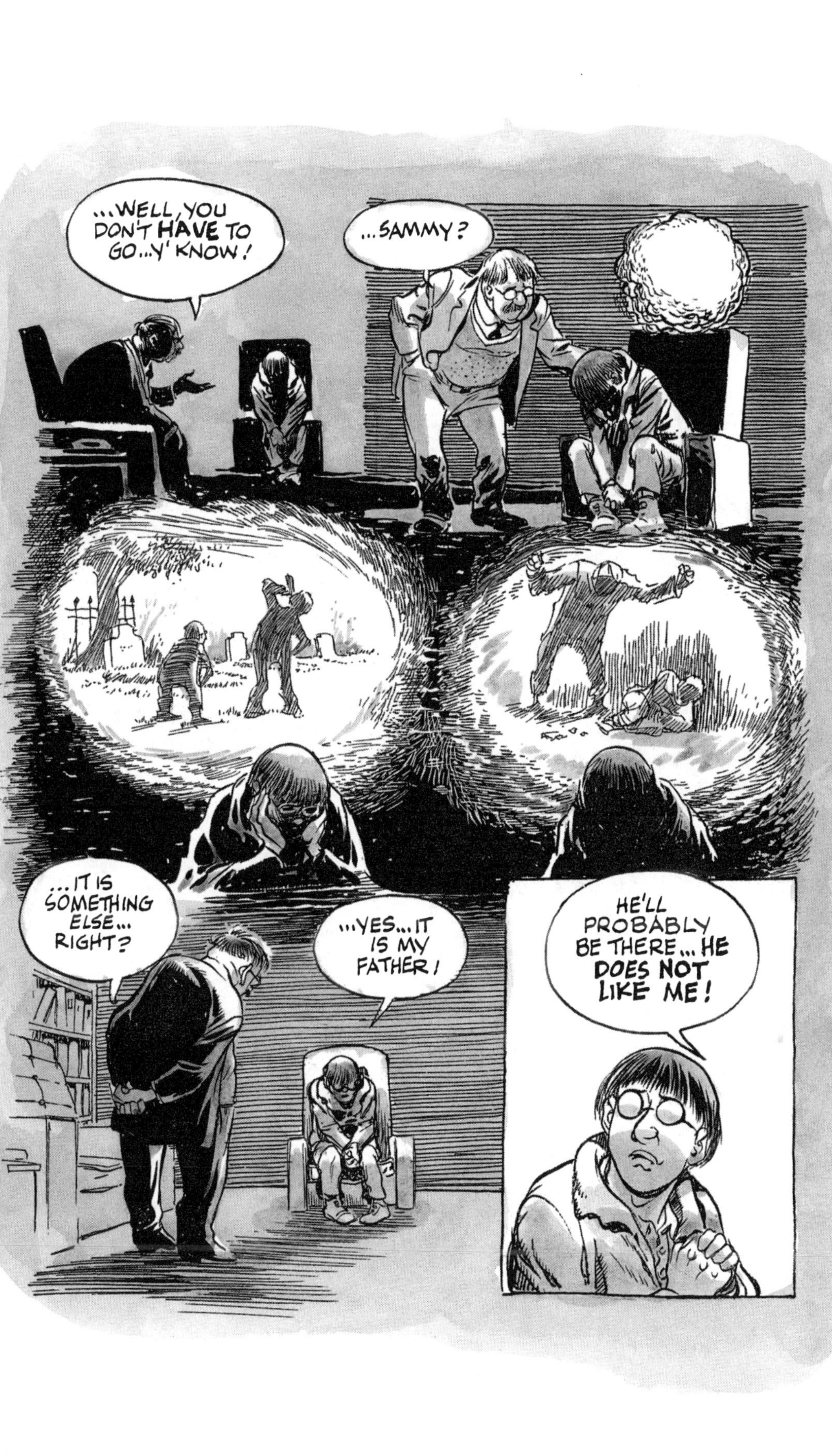
...WELL, YOU DON'T HAVE TO GO...Y' KNOW!
...SAMMY?
...IT IS SOMETHING ELSE... RIGHT?
...YES... IT IS MY FATHER!
HE'LL PROBABLY BE THERE... HE DOES NOT LIKE ME!

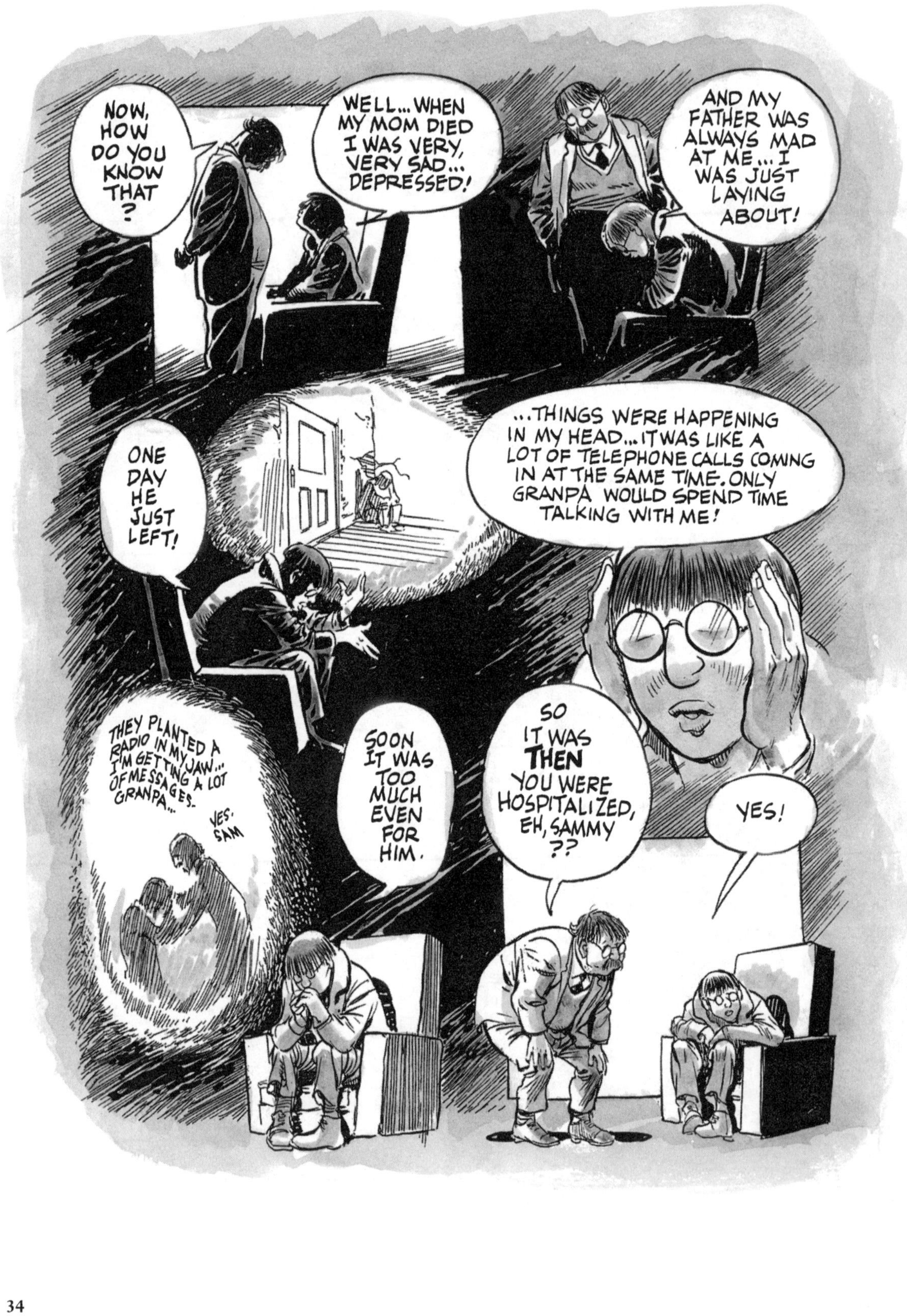
NOW, HOW DO YOU KNOW THAT ?
WELL... WHEN MY MOM DIED I WAS VERY, VERY SAD... DEPRESSED!
AND MY FATHER WAS ALWAYS MAD AT ME... I WAS JUST LAYING ABOUT!
ONE DAY HE JUST LEFT!
...THINGS WERE HAPPENING IN MY HEAD... IT WAS LIKE A LOT OF TELEPHONE CALLS COMING IN AT THE SAME TIME. ONLY GRANPA WOULD SPEND TIME TALKING WITH ME!
THEY PLANTED A RADIO IN MY JAW... I'M GETTING A LOT OF MESSAGES. GRANPA...
YES. SAM
SOON IT WAS TOO MUCH EVEN FOR HIM.
SO IT WAS THEN YOU WERE HOSPITALIZED, EH, SAMMY ??
YES!

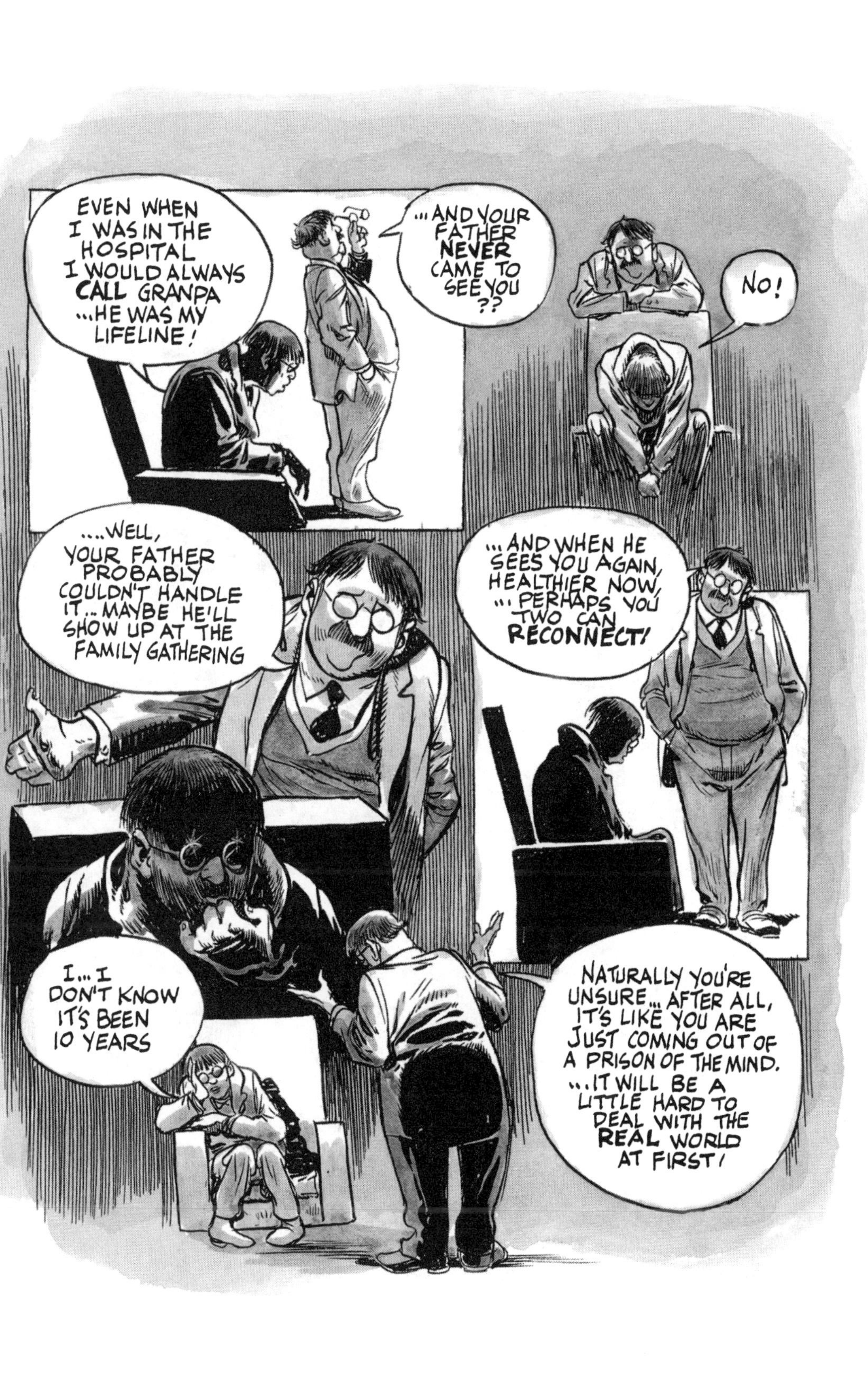
EVEN WHEN I WAS IN THE HOSPITAL I WOULD ALWAYS CALL GRANPA ...HE WAS MY LIFELINE!
...AND YOUR FATHER NEVER CAME TO SEE YOU ??
NO!
....WELL, YOUR FATHER PROBABLY COULDN'T HANDLE IT... MAYBE HE'LL SHOW UP AT THE FAMILY GATHERING
...AND WHEN HE SEES YOU AGAIN, HEALTHIER NOW, ...PERHAPS YOU TWO CAN RECONNECT!
I... I DON'T KNOW IT'S BEEN 10 YEARS
NATURALLY YOU'RE UNSURE... AFTER ALL, IT'S LIKE YOU ARE JUST COMING OUT OF A PRISON OF THE MIND. ...IT WILL BE A LITTLE HARD TO DEAL WITH THE REAL WORLD AT FIRST!

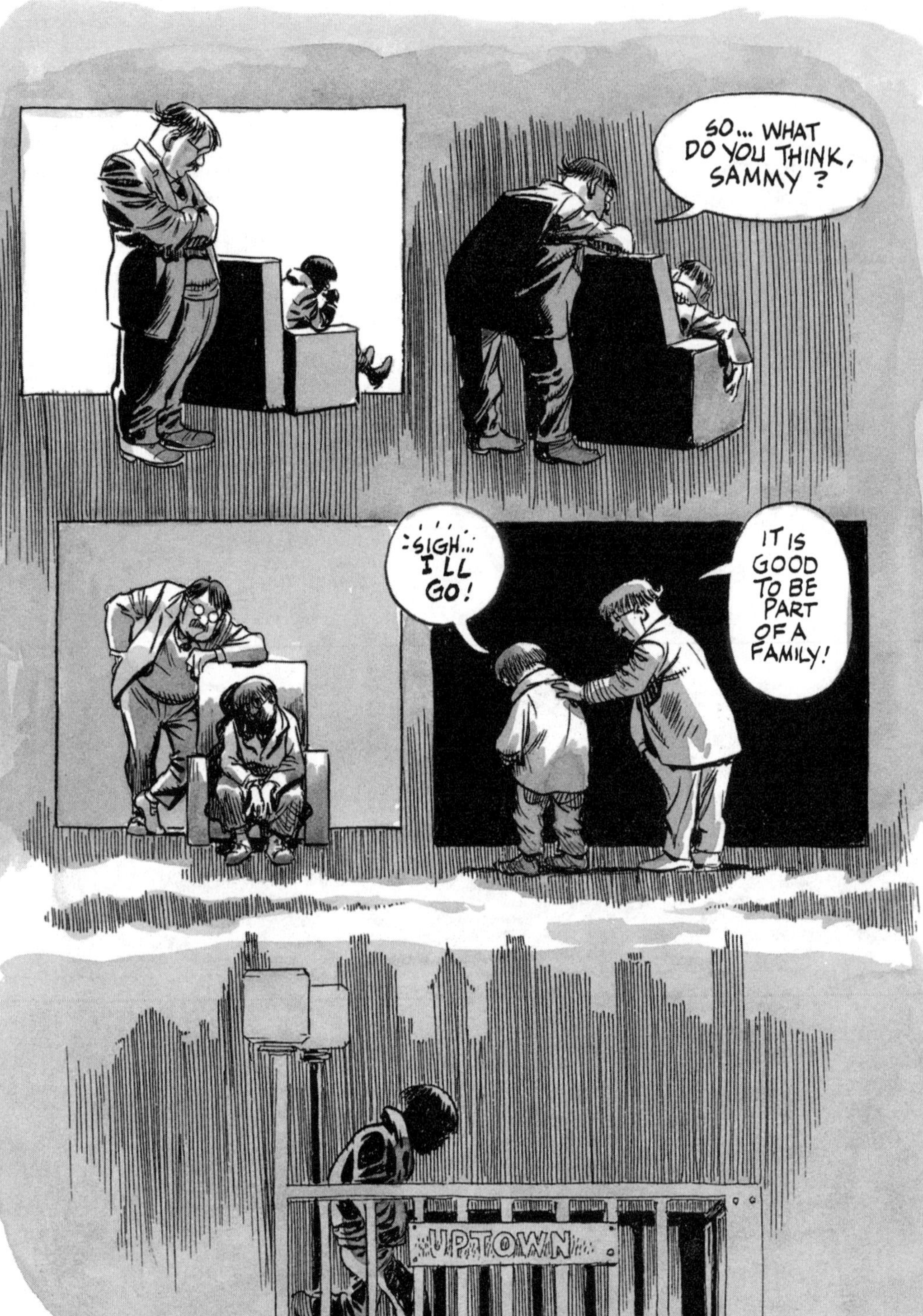
SO... WHAT DO YOU THINK, SAMMY ?
SIGH... I'LL GO!
IT IS GOOD TO BE PART OF A FAMILY!
UPTOWN

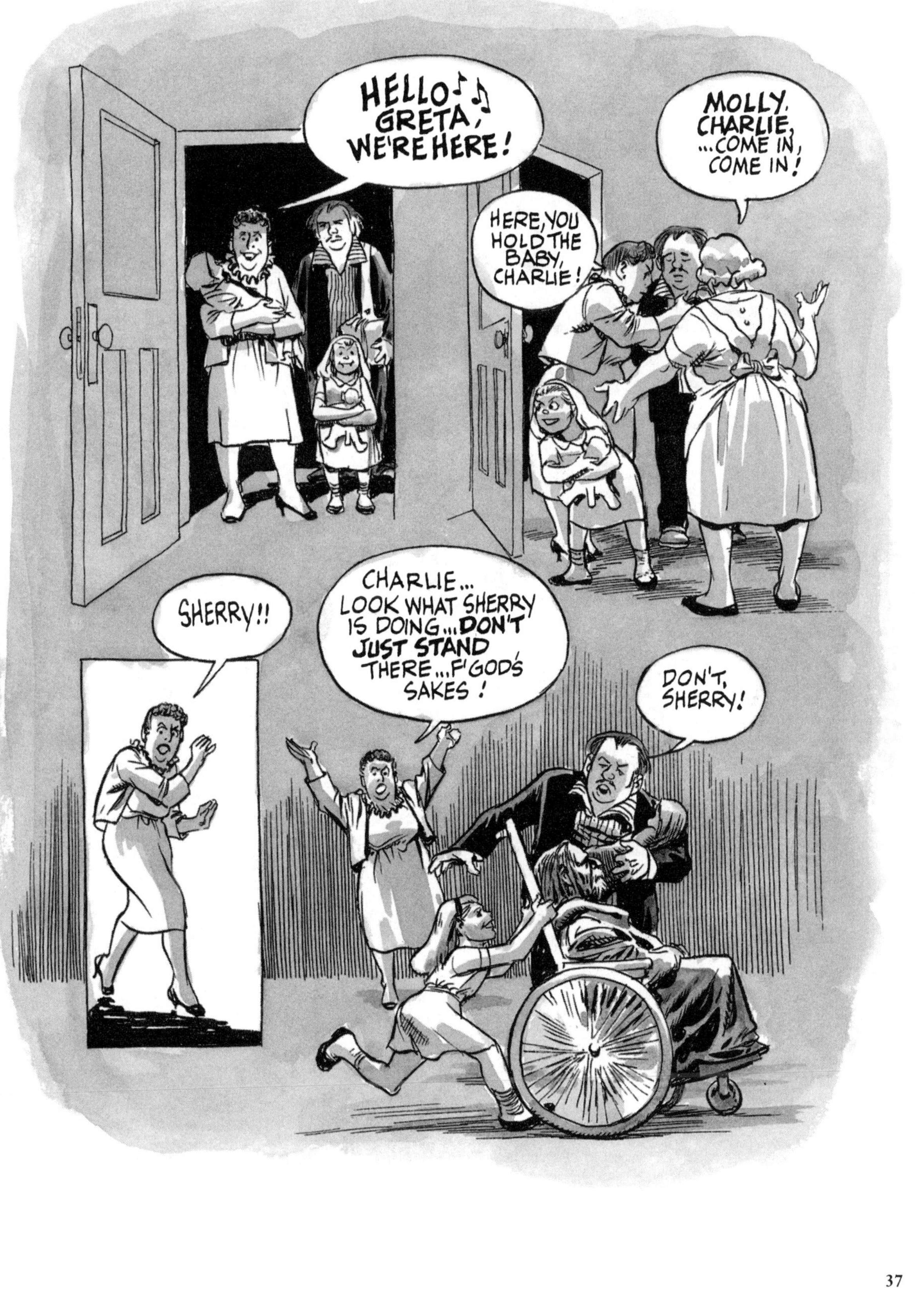
HELLO♪♫ GRETA, WE'RE HERE!
MOLLY, CHARLIE, ...COME IN, COME IN!
HERE, YOU HOLD THE BABY, CHARLIE!
SHERRY!!
CHARLIE... LOOK WHAT SHERRY IS DOING... **DON'T JUST STAND** THERE... F'GOD'S SAKES!
DON'T, SHERRY!

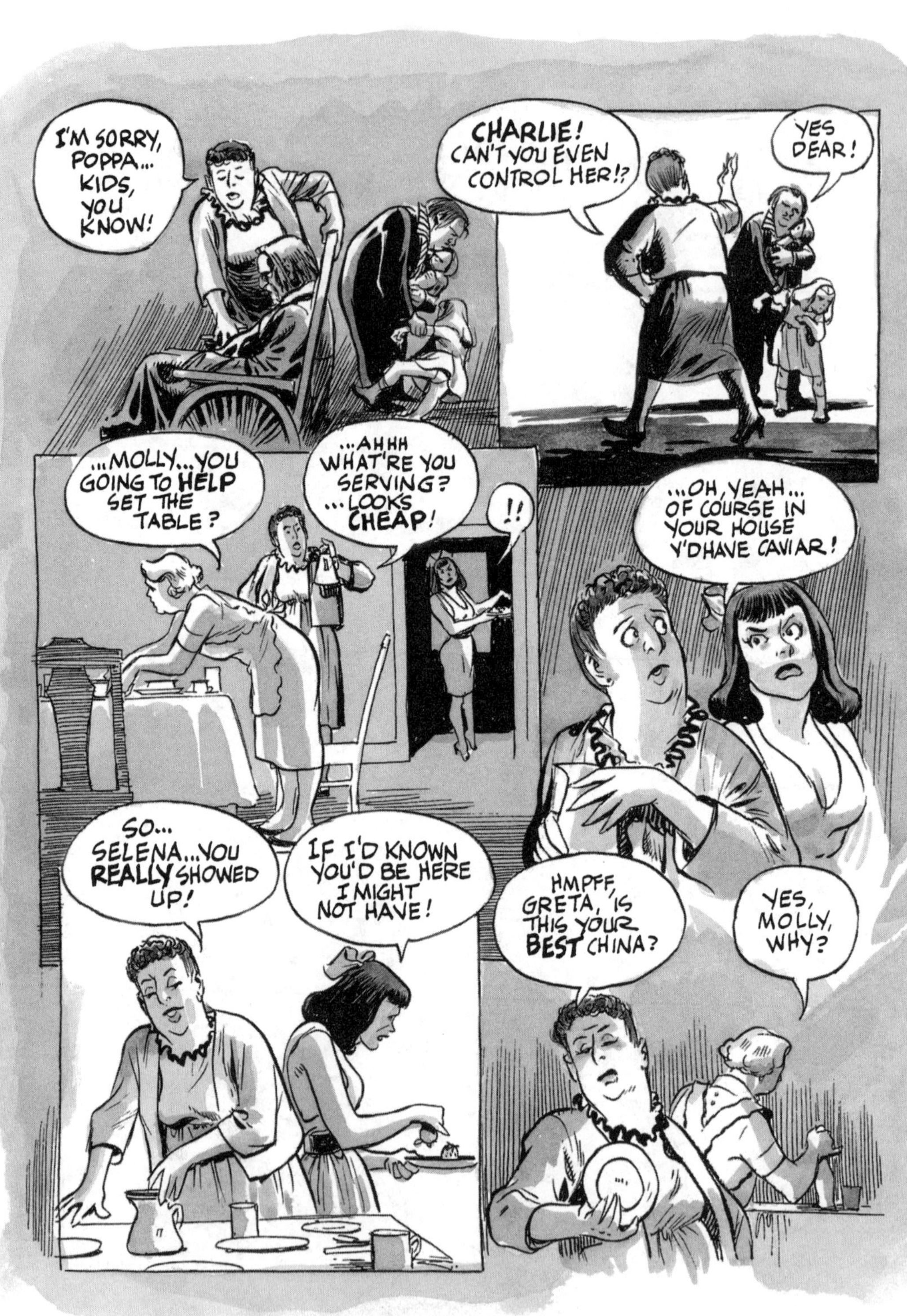
I'M SORRY, POPPA... KIDS, YOU KNOW!
CHARLIE! CAN'T YOU EVEN CONTROL HER!?
YES DEAR!
...MOLLY...YOU GOING TO HELP SET THE TABLE?
...AHHH WHAT'RE YOU SERVING? ...LOOKS CHEAP!
!!
...OH, YEAH... OF COURSE IN YOUR HOUSE Y'DHAVE CAVIAR!
SO... SELENA...YOU REALLY SHOWED UP!
IF I'D KNOWN YOU'D BE HERE I MIGHT NOT HAVE!
HMPFF, GRETA, IS THIS YOUR BEST CHINA?
YES, MOLLY, WHY?

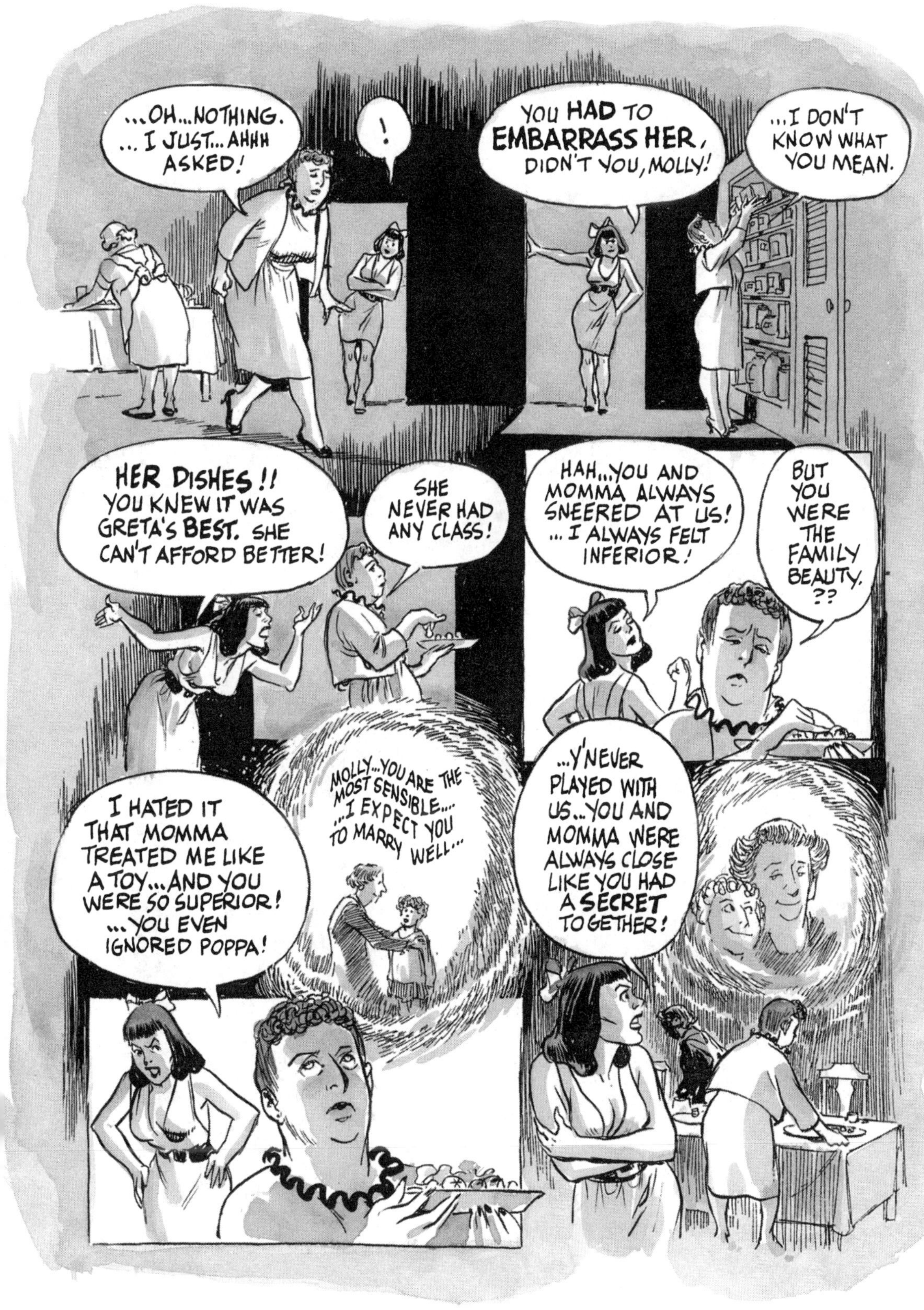
...OH...NOTHING. ... I JUST... AHHH ASKED!
!
YOU HAD TO EMBARRASS HER, DIDN'T YOU, MOLLY!
...I DON'T KNOW WHAT YOU MEAN.
HER DISHES!! YOU KNEW IT WAS GRETA's BEST. SHE CAN'T AFFORD BETTER!
SHE NEVER HAD ANY CLASS!
HAH...YOU AND MOMMA ALWAYS SNEERED AT US! ... I ALWAYS FELT INFERIOR!
BUT YOU WERE THE FAMILY BEAUTY. ??
I HATED IT THAT MOMMA TREATED ME LIKE A TOY...AND YOU WERE SO SUPERIOR! ...YOU EVEN IGNORED POPPA!
MOLLY...YOU ARE THE MOST SENSIBLE.... ...I EXPECT YOU TO MARRY WELL...
...Y'NEVER PLAYED WITH US...YOU AND MOMMA WERE ALWAYS CLOSE LIKE YOU HAD A SECRET TOGETHER!

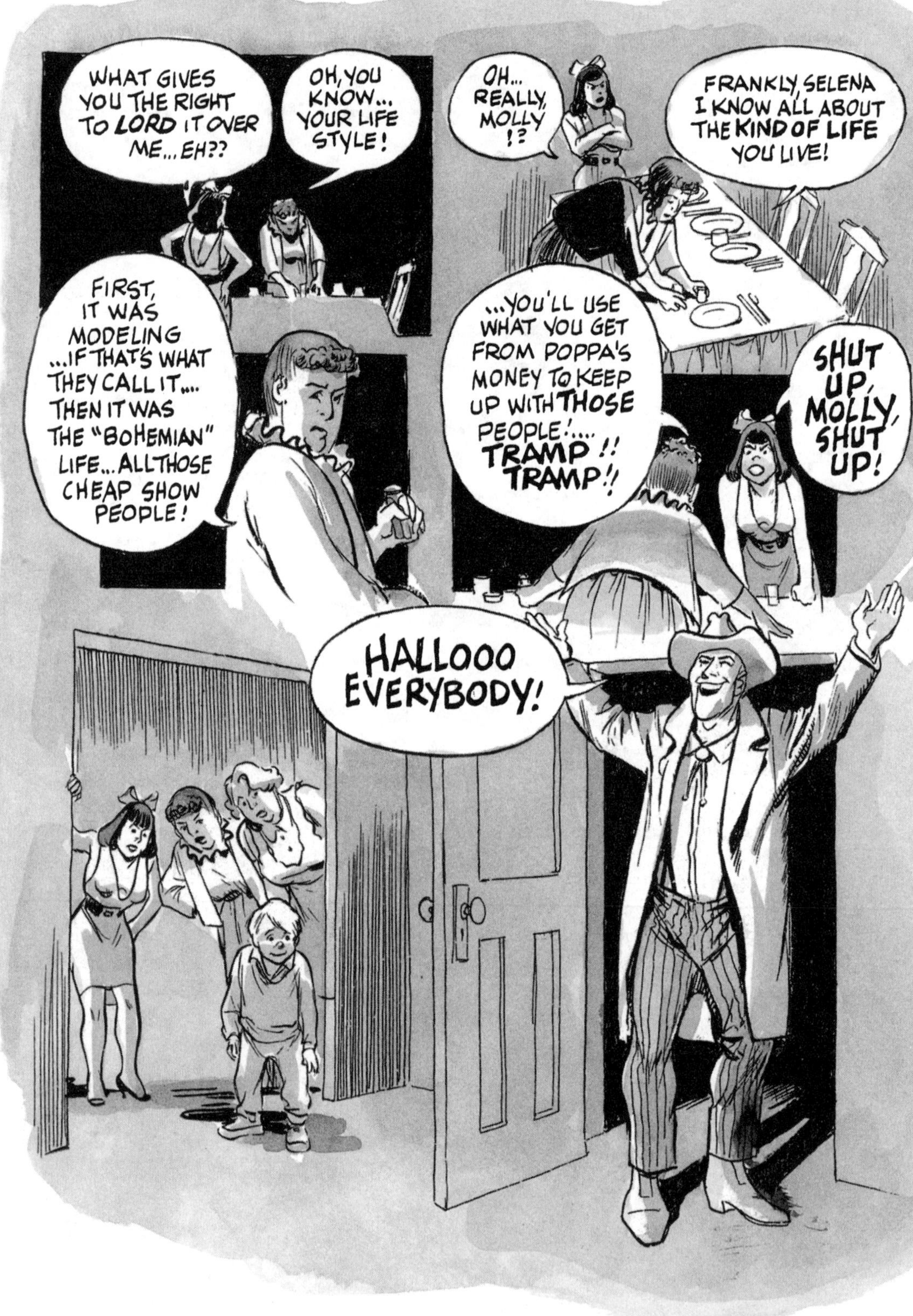
WHAT GIVES YOU THE RIGHT TO LORD IT OVER ME...EH??
OH, YOU KNOW... YOUR LIFE STYLE!
OH... REALLY, MOLLY !?
FRANKLY, SELENA I KNOW ALL ABOUT THE KIND OF LIFE YOU LIVE!
FIRST, IT WAS MODELING ...IF THAT'S WHAT THEY CALL IT.... THEN IT WAS THE "BOHEMIAN" LIFE...ALL THOSE CHEAP SHOW PEOPLE!
...YOU'LL USE WHAT YOU GET FROM POPPA'S MONEY TO KEEP UP WITH THOSE PEOPLE!.... TRAMP!! TRAMP!!
SHUT UP, MOLLY, SHUT UP!
HALLOOO EVERYBODY!

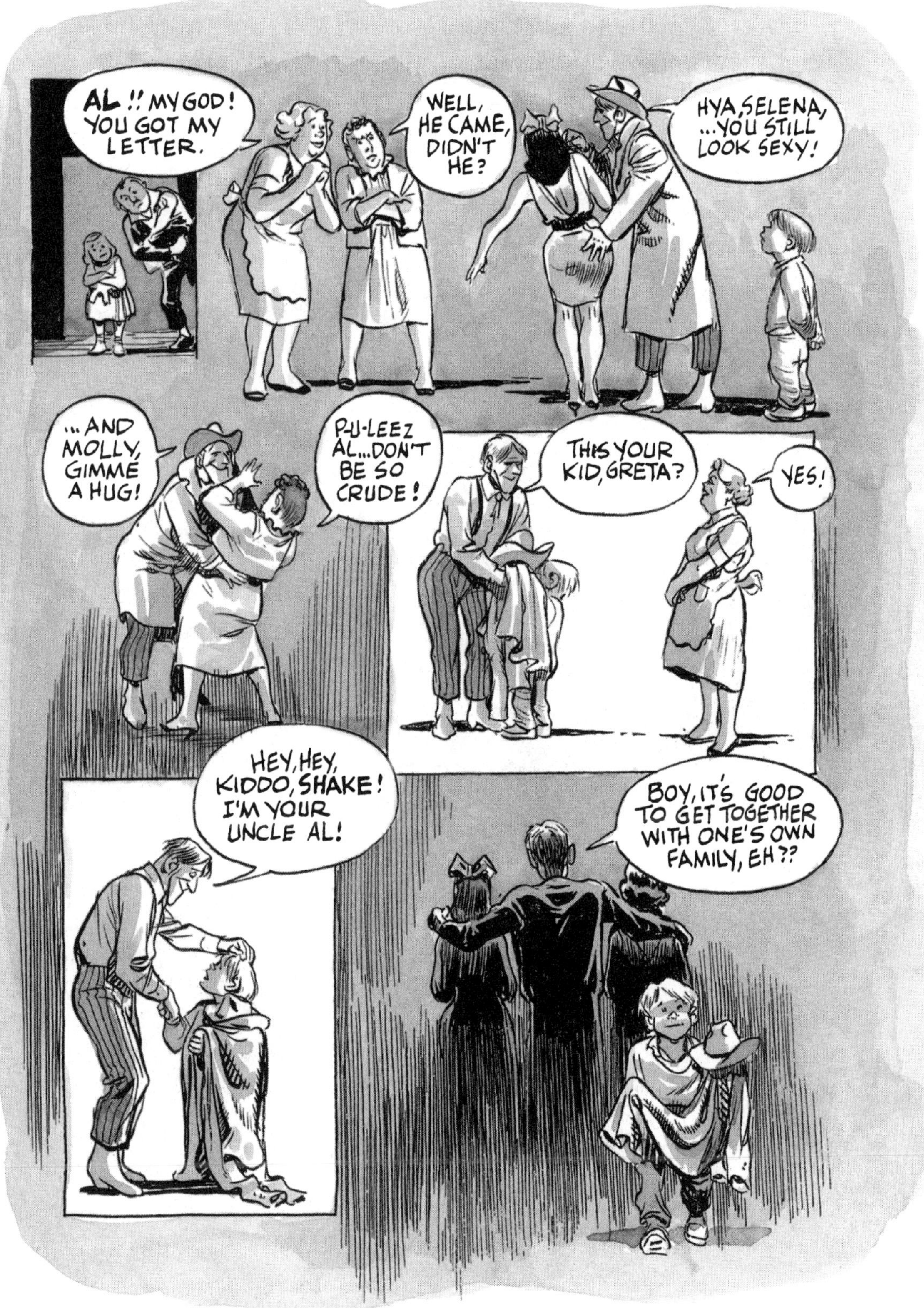
AL!! MY GOD! YOU GOT MY LETTER.
WELL, HE CAME, DIDN'T HE?
HYA, SELENA, ...YOU STILL LOOK SEXY!
...AND MOLLY, GIMME A HUG!
P-U-LEEZ AL...DON'T BE SO CRUDE!
THIS YOUR KID, GRETA?
YES!
HEY, HEY, KIDDO, SHAKE! I'M YOUR UNCLE AL!
BOY, IT'S GOOD TO GET TOGETHER WITH ONE'S OWN FAMILY, EH??

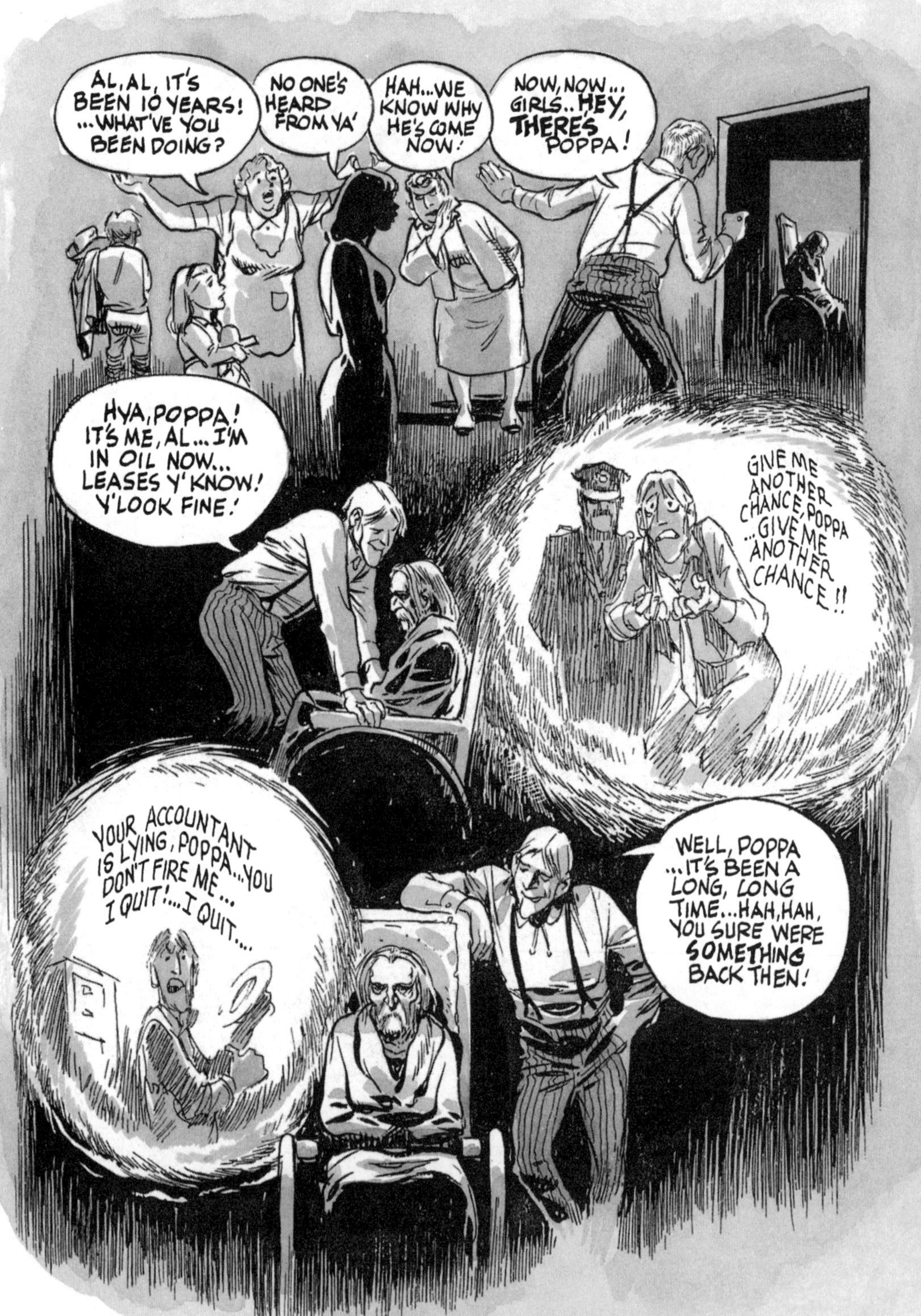
AL, AL, IT'S BEEN 10 YEARS! ...WHAT'VE YOU BEEN DOING?
NO ONE'S HEARD FROM YA'
HAH...WE KNOW WHY HE'S COME NOW!
NOW, NOW... GIRLS.. HEY, THERE'S POPPA!
HYA, POPPA! IT'S ME, AL... I'M IN OIL NOW... LEASES Y'KNOW! Y'LOOK FINE!
GIVE ME ANOTHER CHANCE, POPPA ...GIVE ME ANOTHER CHANCE!!
YOUR ACCOUNTANT IS LYING, POPPA...YOU DON'T FIRE ME... I QUIT!...I QUIT....
WELL, POPPA ...IT'S BEEN A LONG, LONG TIME...HAH, HAH, YOU SURE WERE SOMETHING BACK THEN!

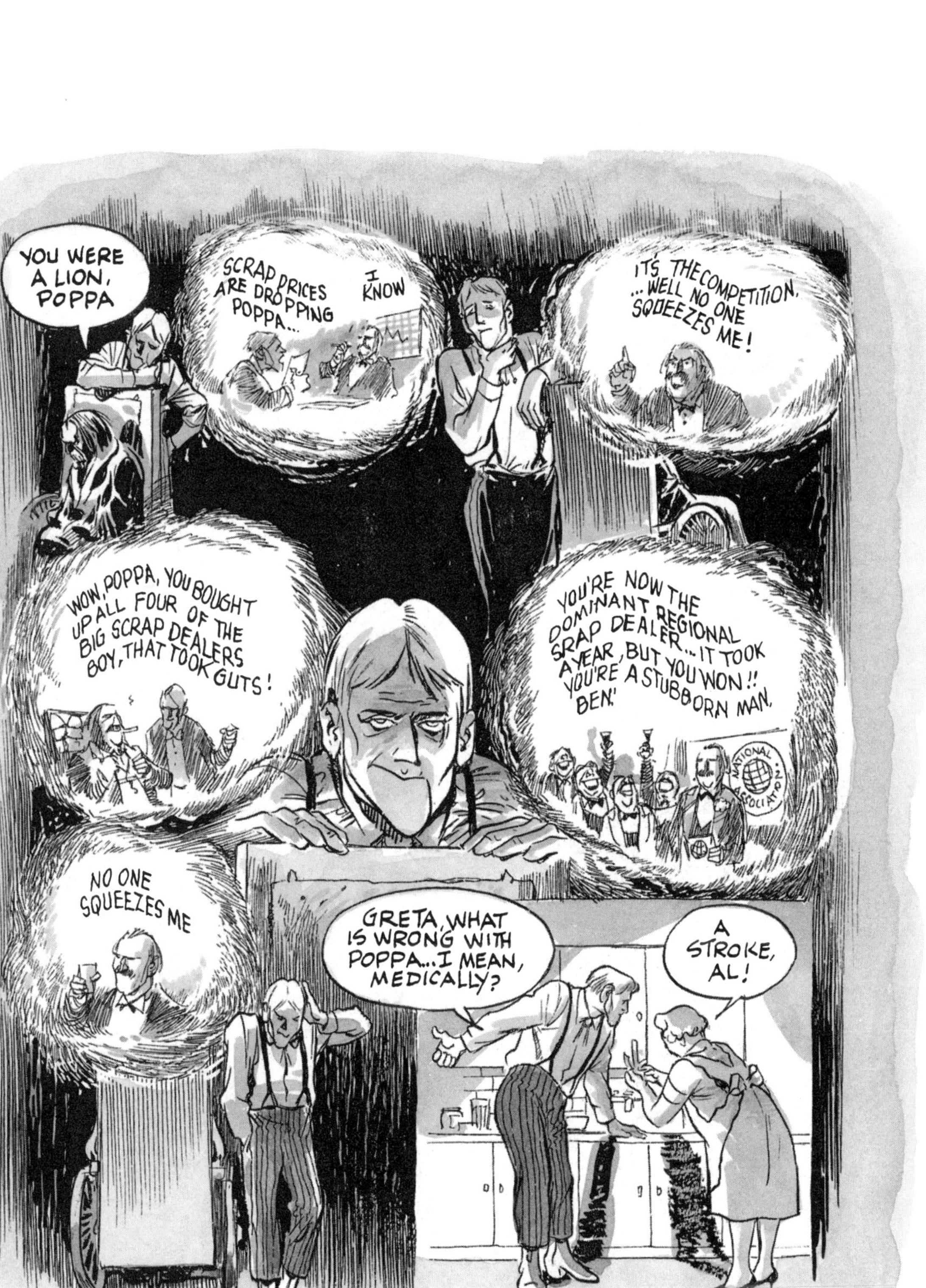
YOU WERE A LION, POPPA
SCRAP PRICES ARE DROPPING POPPA...
I KNOW
IT'S THE COMPETITION, ...WELL NO ONE SQUEEZES ME!
WOW, POPPA, YOU BOUGHT UP ALL FOUR OF THE BIG SCRAP DEALERS
BOY, THAT TOOK GUTS!
YOU'RE NOW THE DOMINANT REGIONAL SRAP DEALER... IT TOOK A YEAR, BUT YOU WON!!
YOU'RE A STUBBORN MAN, BEN.'
NATIONAL ASSOCIATION
NO ONE SQUEEZES ME
GRETA, WHAT IS WRONG WITH POPPA...I MEAN, MEDICALLY?
A STROKE, AL!

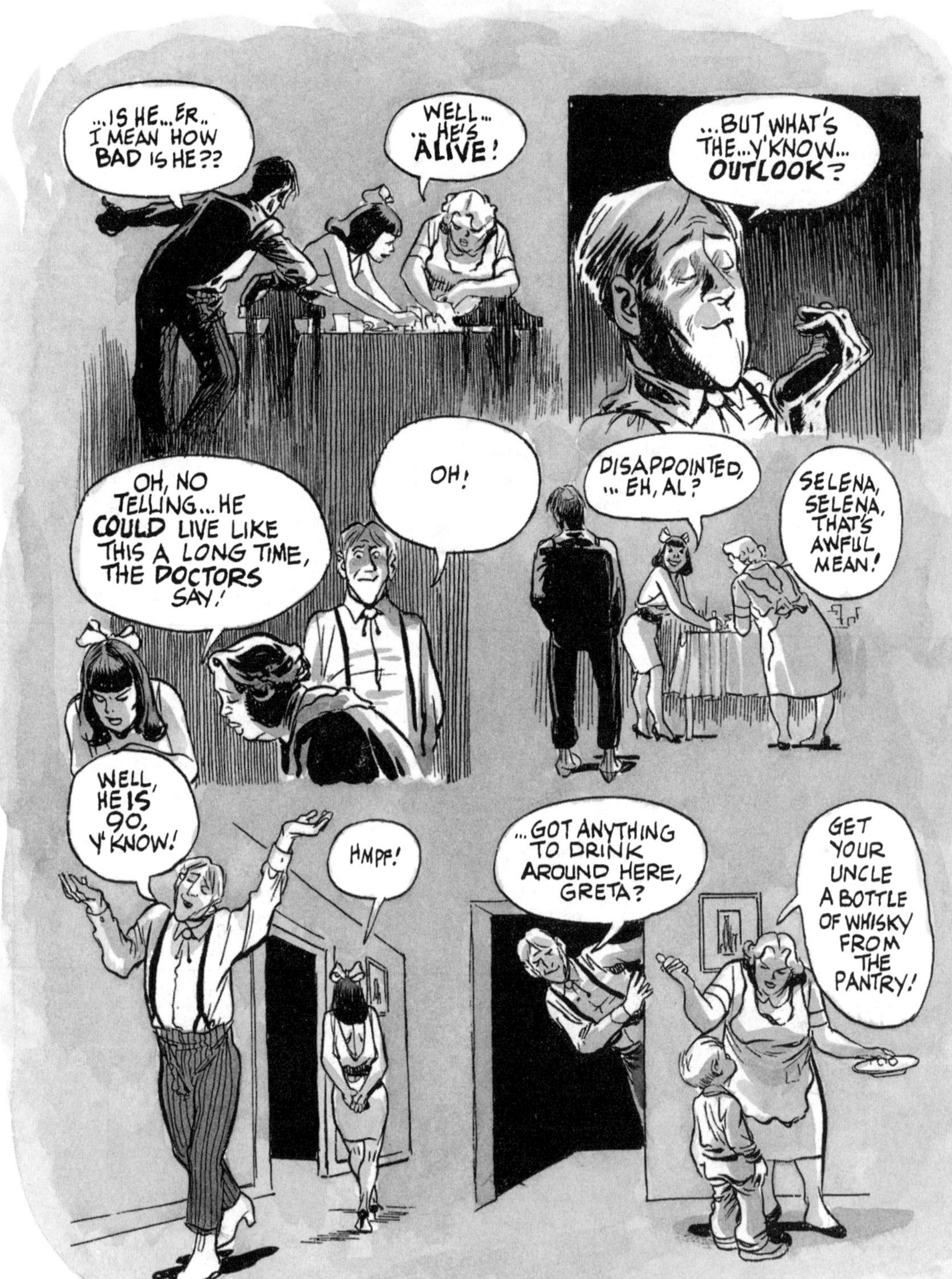
...IS HE...ER.. I MEAN HOW BAD IS HE??
WELL... ...HE'S ALIVE!
...BUT WHAT'S THE...Y'KNOW... OUTLOOK?
OH, NO TELLING... HE COULD LIVE LIKE THIS A LONG TIME, THE DOCTORS SAY!
OH!
DISAPPOINTED, ... EH, AL?
SELENA, SELENA, THAT'S AWFUL MEAN!
WELL, HE IS 90, Y'KNOW!
HMPF!
...GOT ANYTHING TO DRINK AROUND HERE, GRETA?
GET YOUR UNCLE A BOTTLE OF WHISKY FROM THE PANTRY!

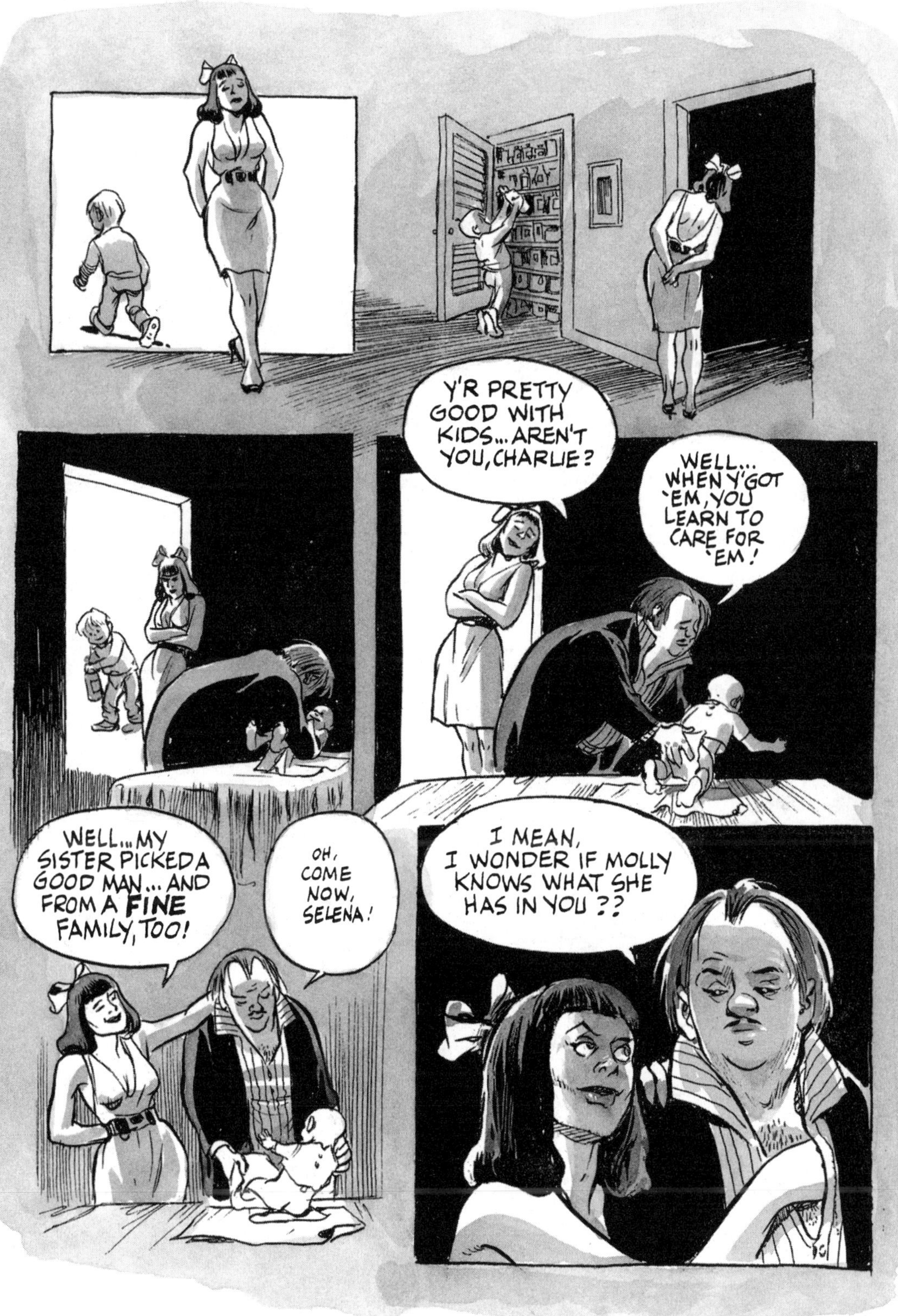
Y'R PRETTY GOOD WITH KIDS... AREN'T YOU, CHARLIE?
WELL... WHEN Y'GOT 'EM, YOU LEARN TO CARE FOR 'EM!
WELL... MY SISTER PICKED A GOOD MAN... AND FROM A FINE FAMILY, TOO!
OH, COME NOW, SELENA!
I MEAN, I WONDER IF MOLLY KNOWS WHAT SHE HAS IN YOU??

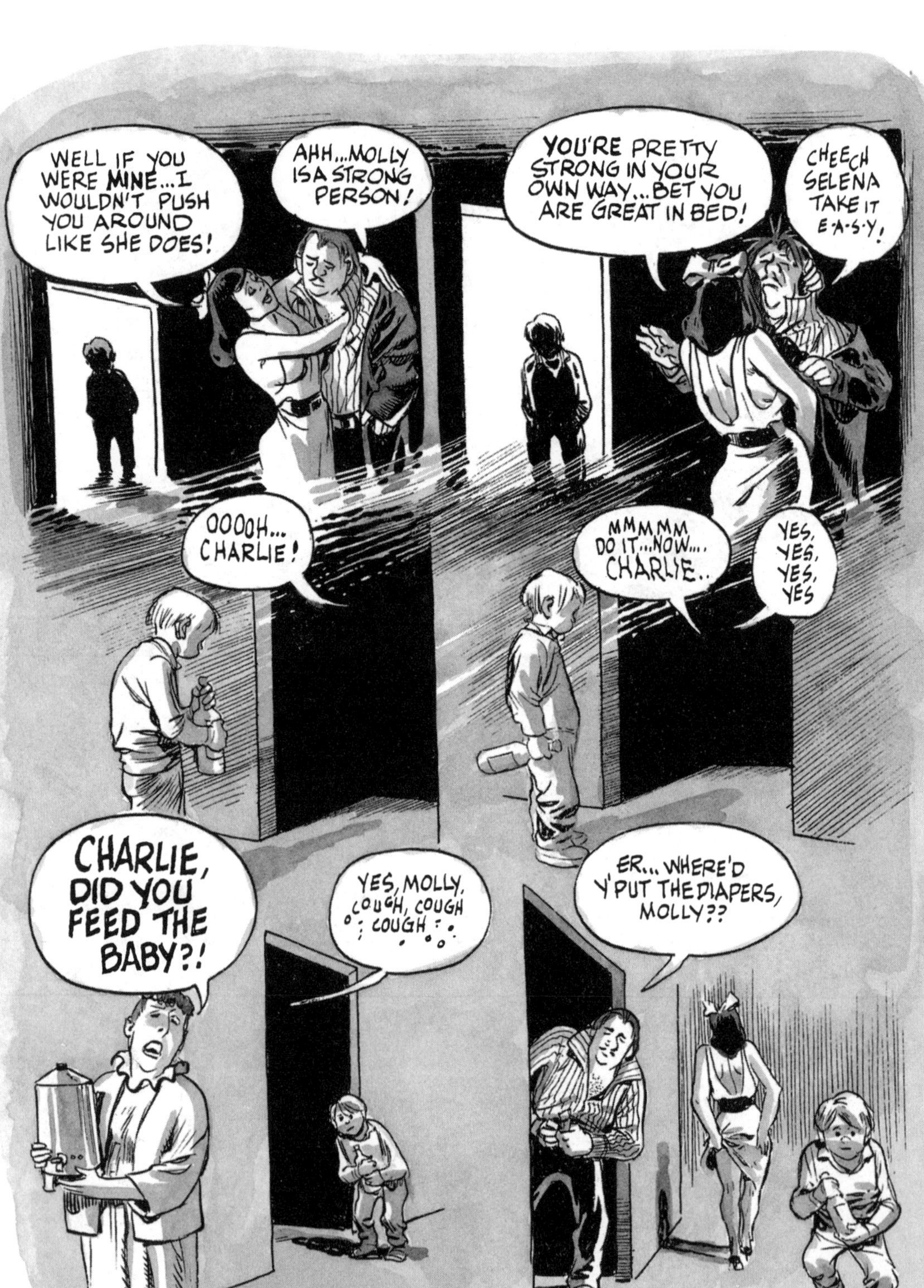
WELL IF YOU WERE MINE...I WOULDN'T PUSH YOU AROUND LIKE SHE DOES!
AHH...MOLLY IS A STRONG PERSON!
YOU'RE PRETTY STRONG IN YOUR OWN WAY...BET YOU ARE GREAT IN BED!
CHEECH SELENA TAKE IT E-A-S-Y!
OOOOH... CHARLIE!
MMMMM DO IT...NOW.... CHARLIE..
YES, YES, YES, YES
CHARLIE, DID YOU FEED THE BABY?!
YES, MOLLY, COUGH, COUGH COUGH
ER... WHERE'D Y'PUT THE DIAPERS, MOLLY??

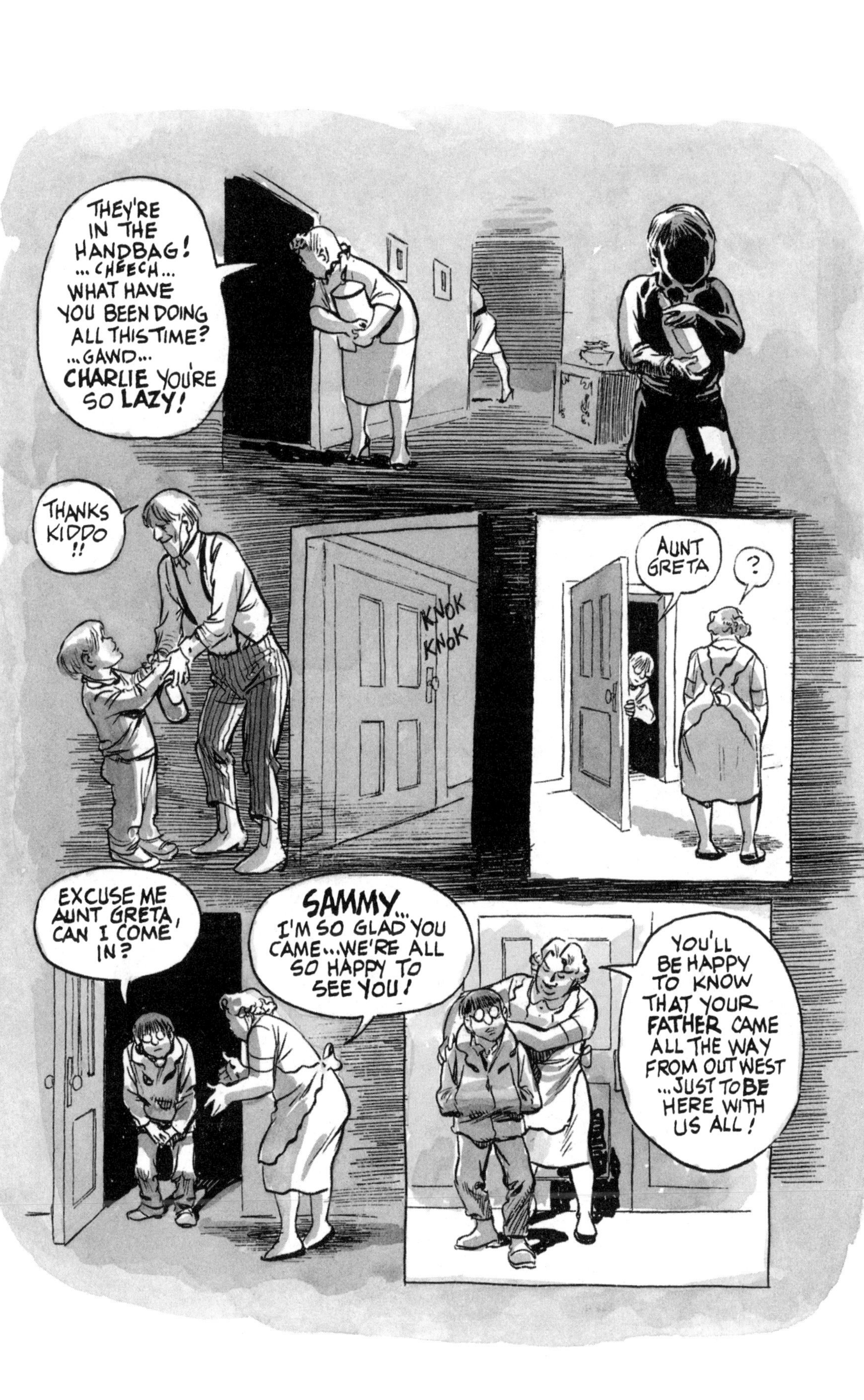
THEY'RE IN THE HANDBAG! ...CHEECH... WHAT HAVE YOU BEEN DOING ALL THIS TIME? ...GAWD... CHARLIE YOU'RE SO LAZY!
THANKS KIDDO !!
KNOK KNOK
AUNT GRETA
?
EXCUSE ME AUNT GRETA, CAN I COME IN?
SAMMY... I'M SO GLAD YOU CAME...WE'RE ALL SO HAPPY TO SEE YOU!
YOU'LL BE HAPPY TO KNOW THAT YOUR FATHER CAME ALL THE WAY FROM OUT WEST ...JUST TO BE HERE WITH US ALL!

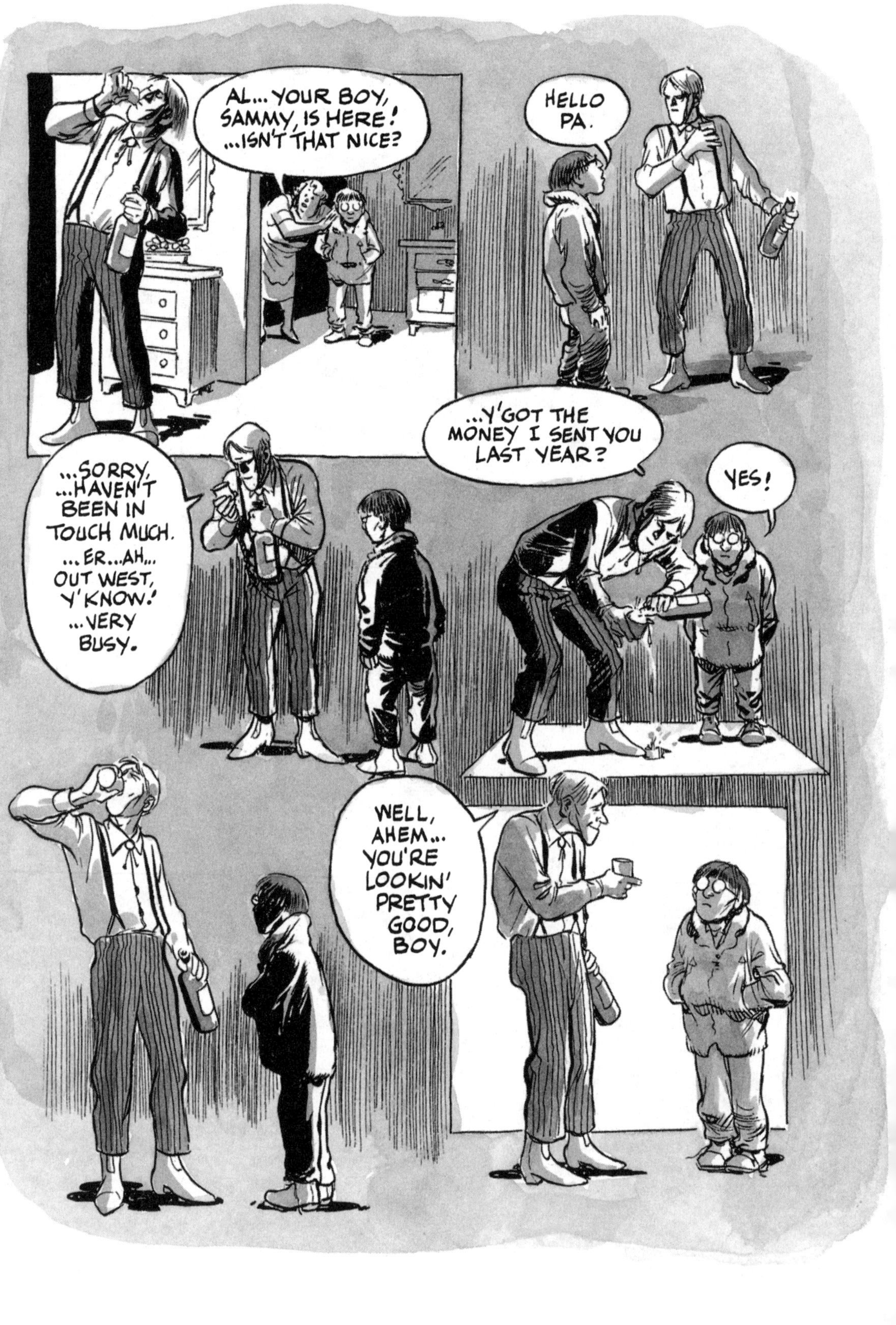
AL... YOUR BOY, SAMMY, IS HERE! ...ISN'T THAT NICE?
HELLO PA.
...Y'GOT THE MONEY I SENT YOU LAST YEAR?
YES!
...SORRY, ...HAVEN'T BEEN IN TOUCH MUCH. ...ER...AH... OUT WEST, Y'KNOW! ...VERY BUSY.
WELL, AHEM... YOU'RE LOOKIN' PRETTY GOOD, BOY.

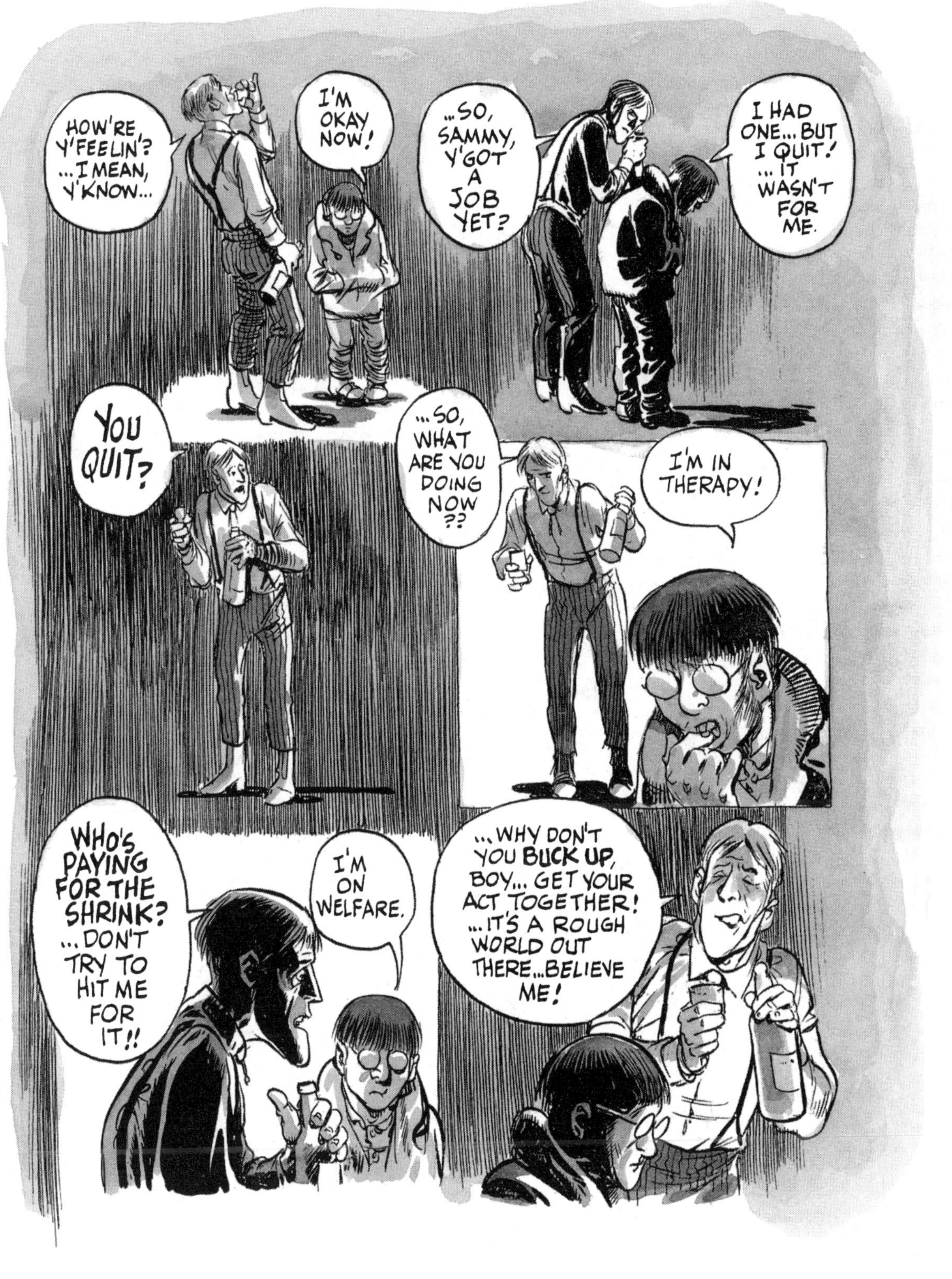
HOW'RE Y'FEELIN'? ...I MEAN, Y'KNOW...
I'M OKAY NOW!
...SO, SAMMY, Y'GOT A JOB YET?
I HAD ONE... BUT I QUIT! ...IT WASN'T FOR ME.
YOU QUIT?
...SO, WHAT ARE YOU DOING NOW??
I'M IN THERAPY!
WHO'S PAYING FOR THE SHRINK? ...DON'T TRY TO HIT ME FOR IT!!
I'M ON WELFARE.
...WHY DON'T YOU BUCK UP, BOY... GET YOUR ACT TOGETHER! ...IT'S A ROUGH WORLD OUT THERE...BELIEVE ME!

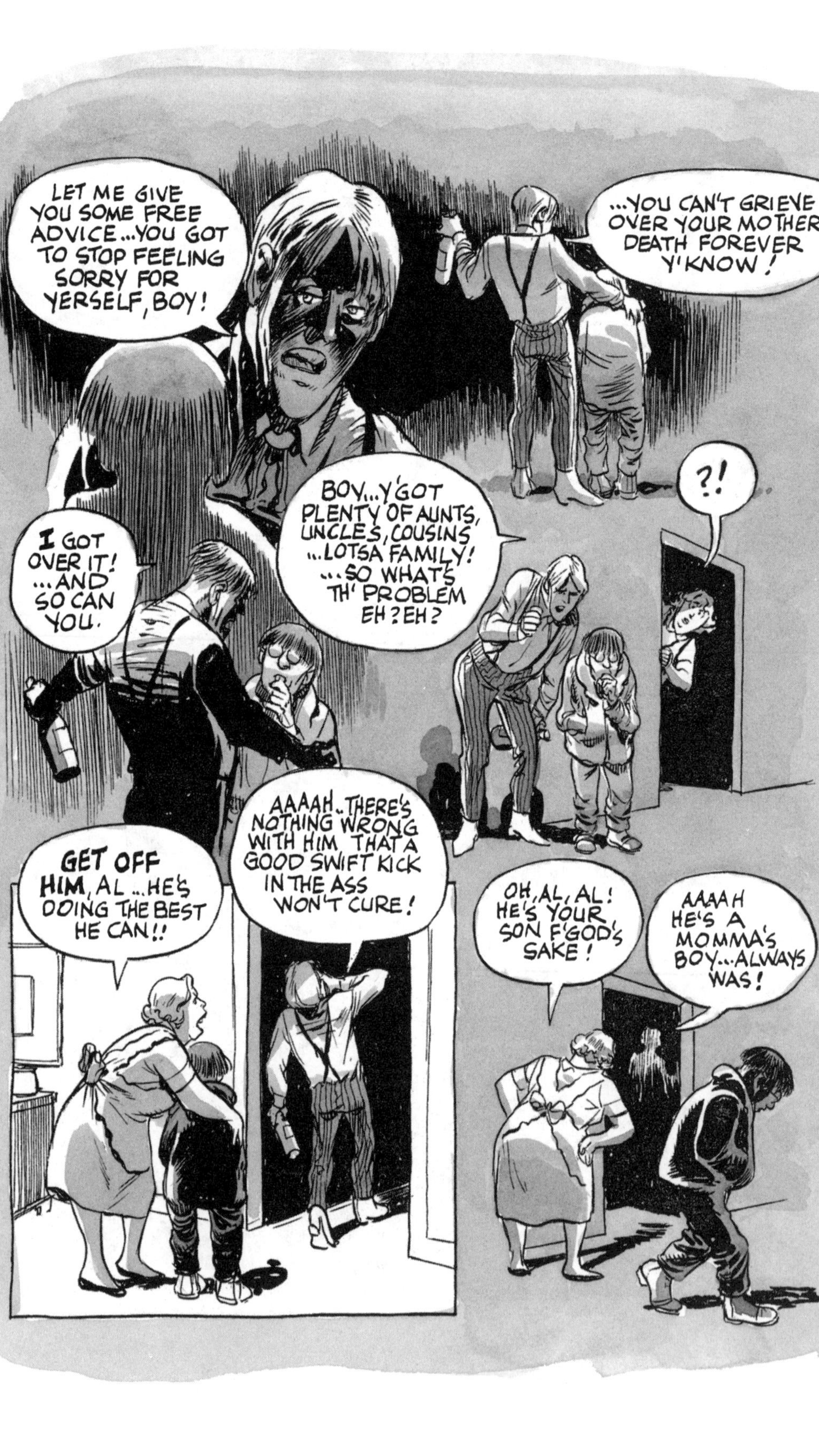
LET ME GIVE YOU SOME FREE ADVICE...YOU GOT TO STOP FEELING SORRY FOR YERSELF, BOY!
...YOU CAN'T GRIEVE OVER YOUR MOTHER'S DEATH FOREVER Y'KNOW!
I GOT OVER IT! ...AND SO CAN YOU.
BOY...Y'GOT PLENTY OF AUNTS, UNCLES, COUSINS ...LOTSA FAMILY! ...SO WHAT'S TH' PROBLEM EH? EH?
?!
GET OFF HIM, AL...HE'S DOING THE BEST HE CAN!!
AAAAH..THERE'S NOTHING WRONG WITH HIM THAT A GOOD SWIFT KICK IN THE ASS WON'T CURE!
OH, AL, AL! HE'S YOUR SON F'GOD'S SAKE!
AAAAH HE'S A MOMMA'S BOY...ALWAYS WAS!

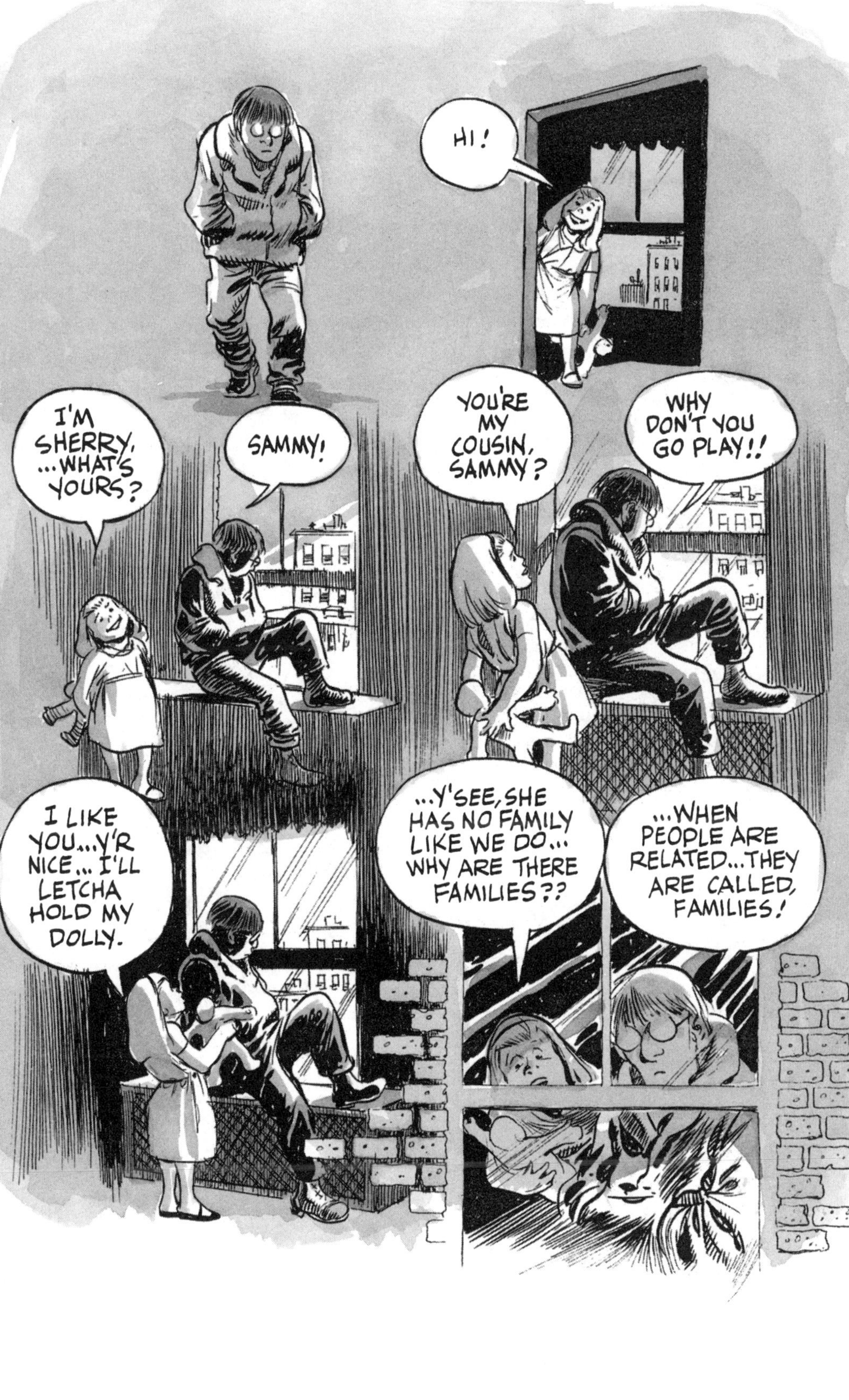
HI!
I'M SHERRY, ...WHAT'S YOURS?
SAMMY!
YOU'RE MY COUSIN, SAMMY?
WHY DON'T YOU GO PLAY!!
I LIKE YOU...Y'R NICE... I'LL LETCHA HOLD MY DOLLY.
...Y'SEE, SHE HAS NO FAMILY LIKE WE DO... WHY ARE THERE FAMILIES??
...WHEN PEOPLE ARE RELATED...THEY ARE CALLED, FAMILIES!

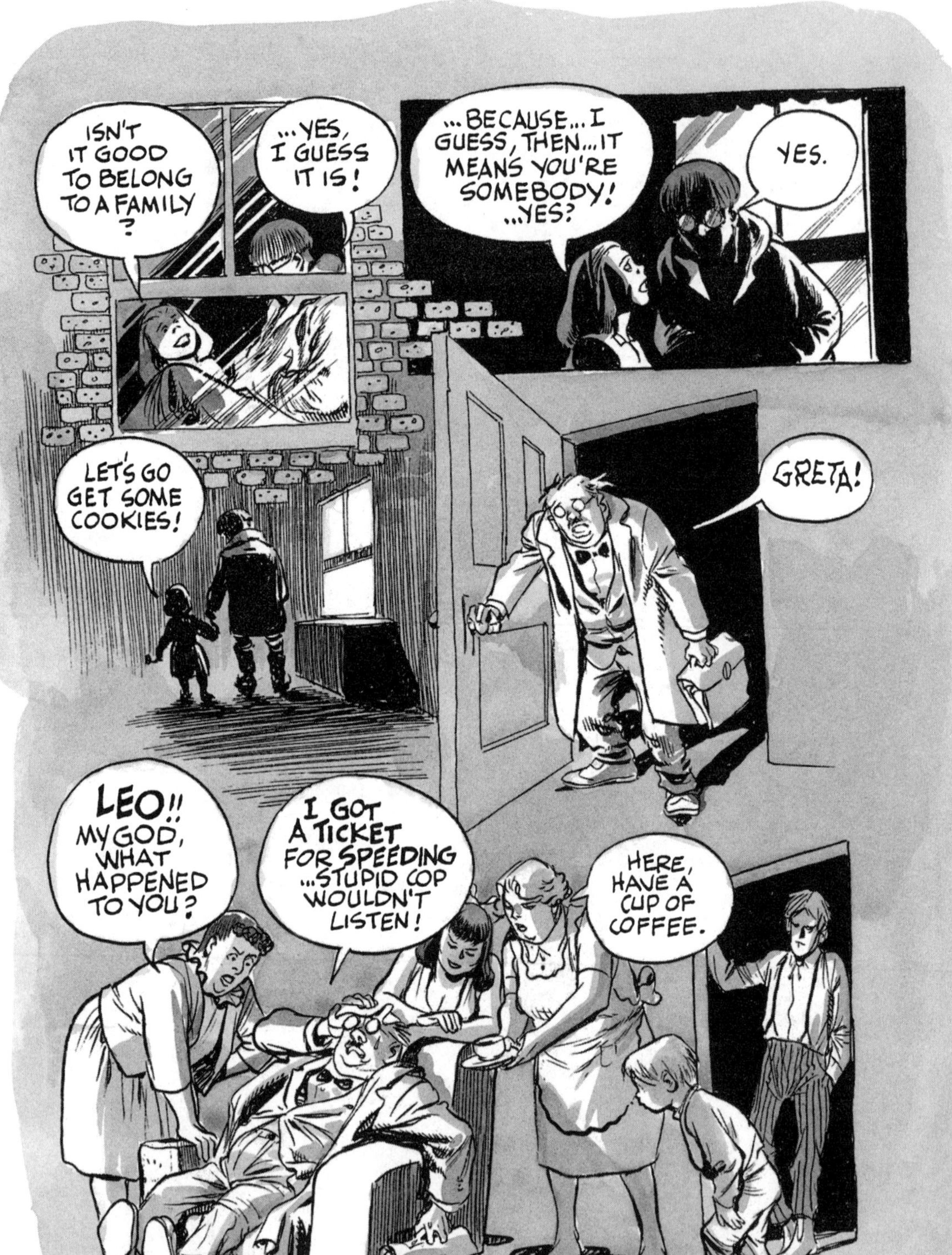
ISN'T IT GOOD TO BELONG TO A FAMILY ?
...YES, I GUESS IT IS!
...BECAUSE... I GUESS, THEN... IT MEANS YOU'RE SOMEBODY! ...YES?
YES.
LET'S GO GET SOME COOKIES!
GRETA!
LEO!! MY GOD, WHAT HAPPENED TO YOU?
I GOT A TICKET FOR SPEEDING ...STUPID COP WOULDN'T LISTEN!
HERE, HAVE A CUP OF COFFEE.

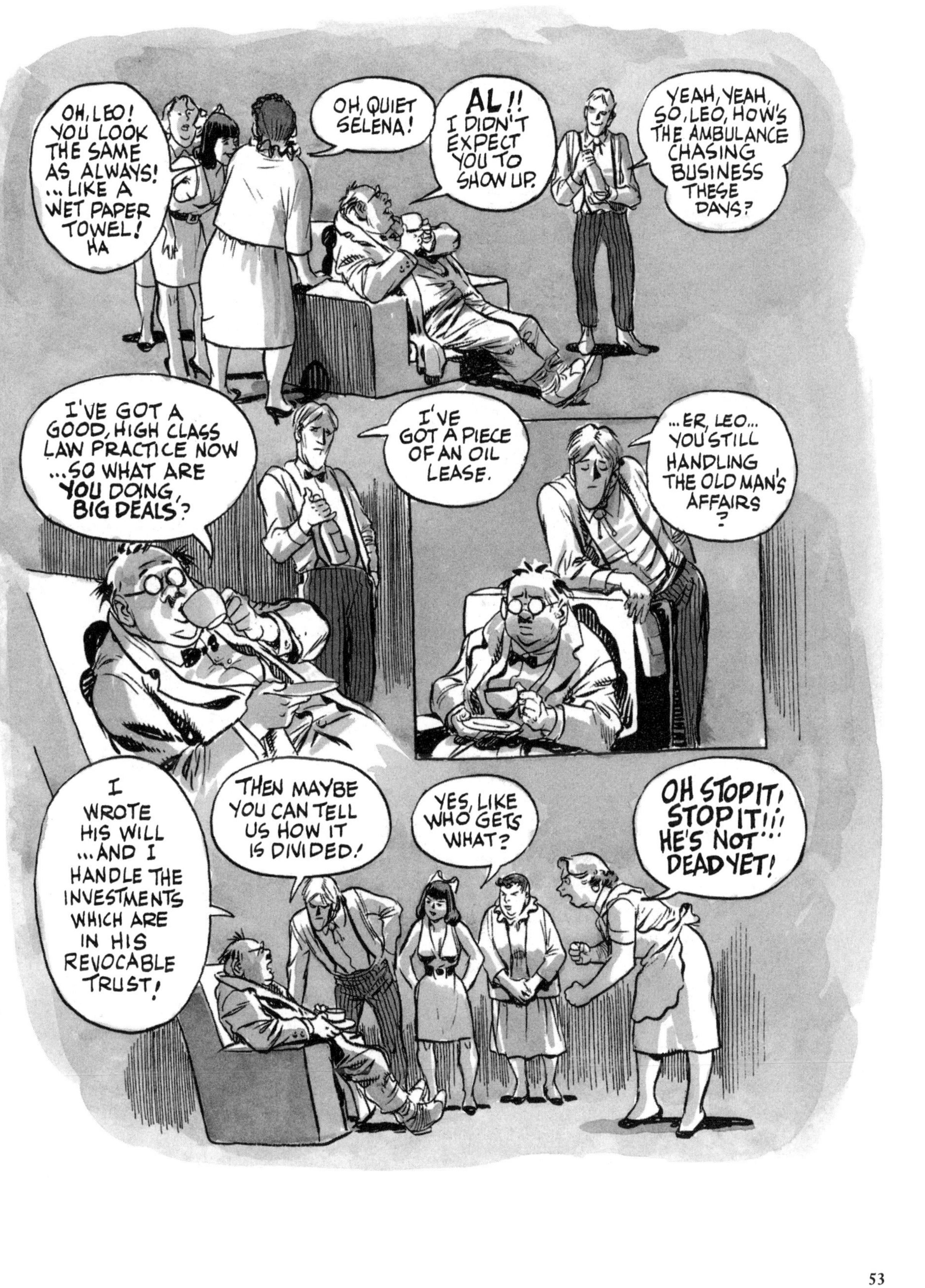
OH, LEO! YOU LOOK THE SAME AS ALWAYS! ...LIKE A WET PAPER TOWEL! HA
OH, QUIET SELENA!
AL!! I DIDN'T EXPECT YOU TO SHOW UP.
YEAH, YEAH, SO, LEO, HOW'S THE AMBULANCE CHASING BUSINESS THESE DAYS?
I'VE GOT A GOOD, HIGH CLASS LAW PRACTICE NOW ...SO WHAT ARE YOU DOING, BIG DEALS?
I'VE GOT A PIECE OF AN OIL LEASE.
...ER, LEO... YOU'STILL HANDLING THE OLD MAN'S AFFAIRS?
I WROTE HIS WILL ...AND I HANDLE THE INVESTMENTS WHICH ARE IN HIS REVOCABLE TRUST!
THEN MAYBE YOU CAN TELL US HOW IT IS DIVIDED!
YES, LIKE WHO GETS WHAT?
OH STOP IT, STOP IT!!! HE'S NOT... DEAD YET!

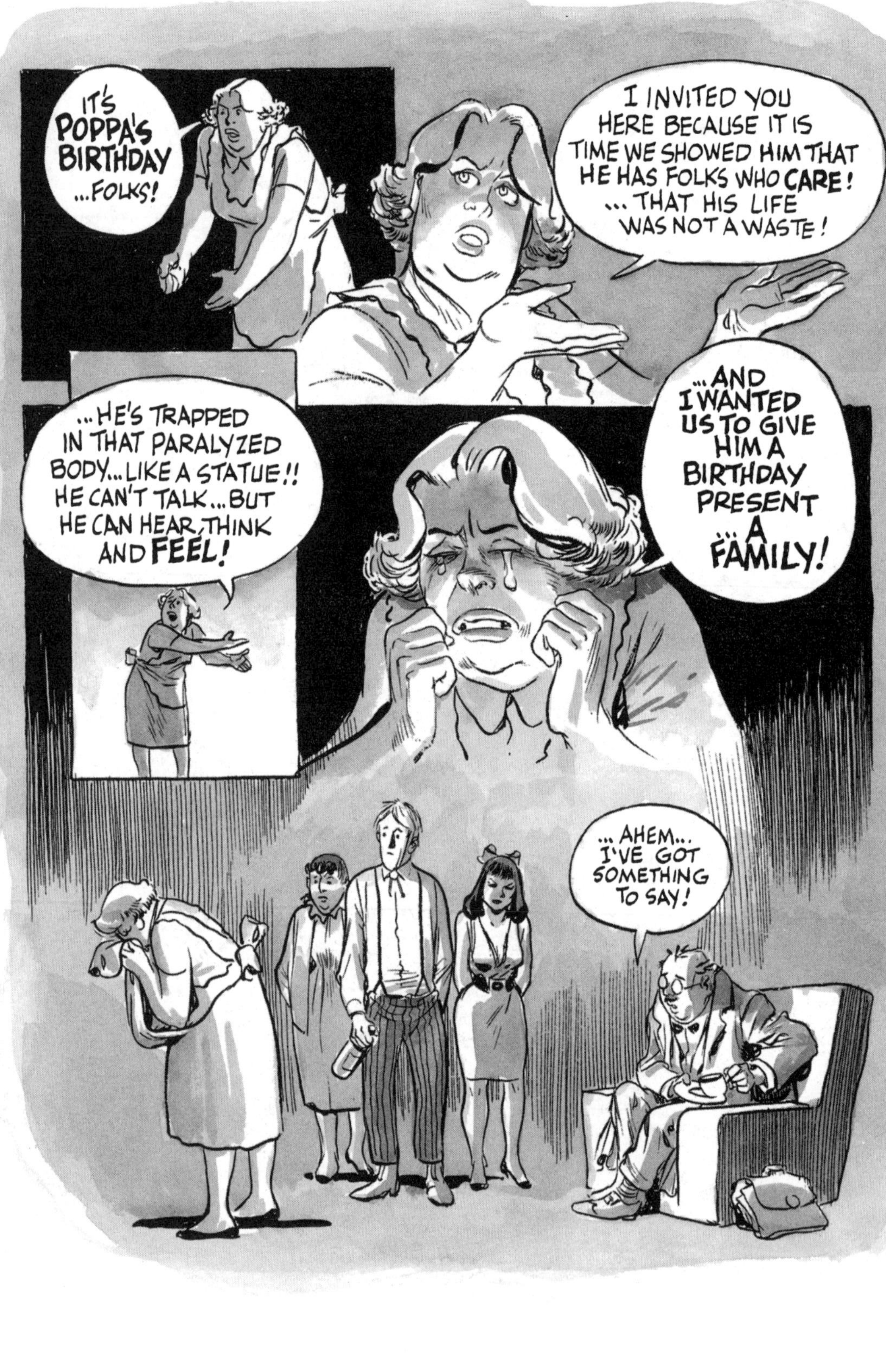
IT'S POPPA'S BIRTHDAY ...FOLKS!
I INVITED YOU HERE BECAUSE IT IS TIME WE SHOWED HIM THAT HE HAS FOLKS WHO CARE! ... THAT HIS LIFE WAS NOT A WASTE!
...HE'S TRAPPED IN THAT PARALYZED BODY... LIKE A STATUE!! HE CAN'T TALK... BUT HE CAN HEAR, THINK AND FEEL!
...AND I WANTED US TO GIVE HIM A BIRTHDAY PRESENT ...A FAMILY!
...AHEM... I'VE GOT SOMETHING TO SAY!

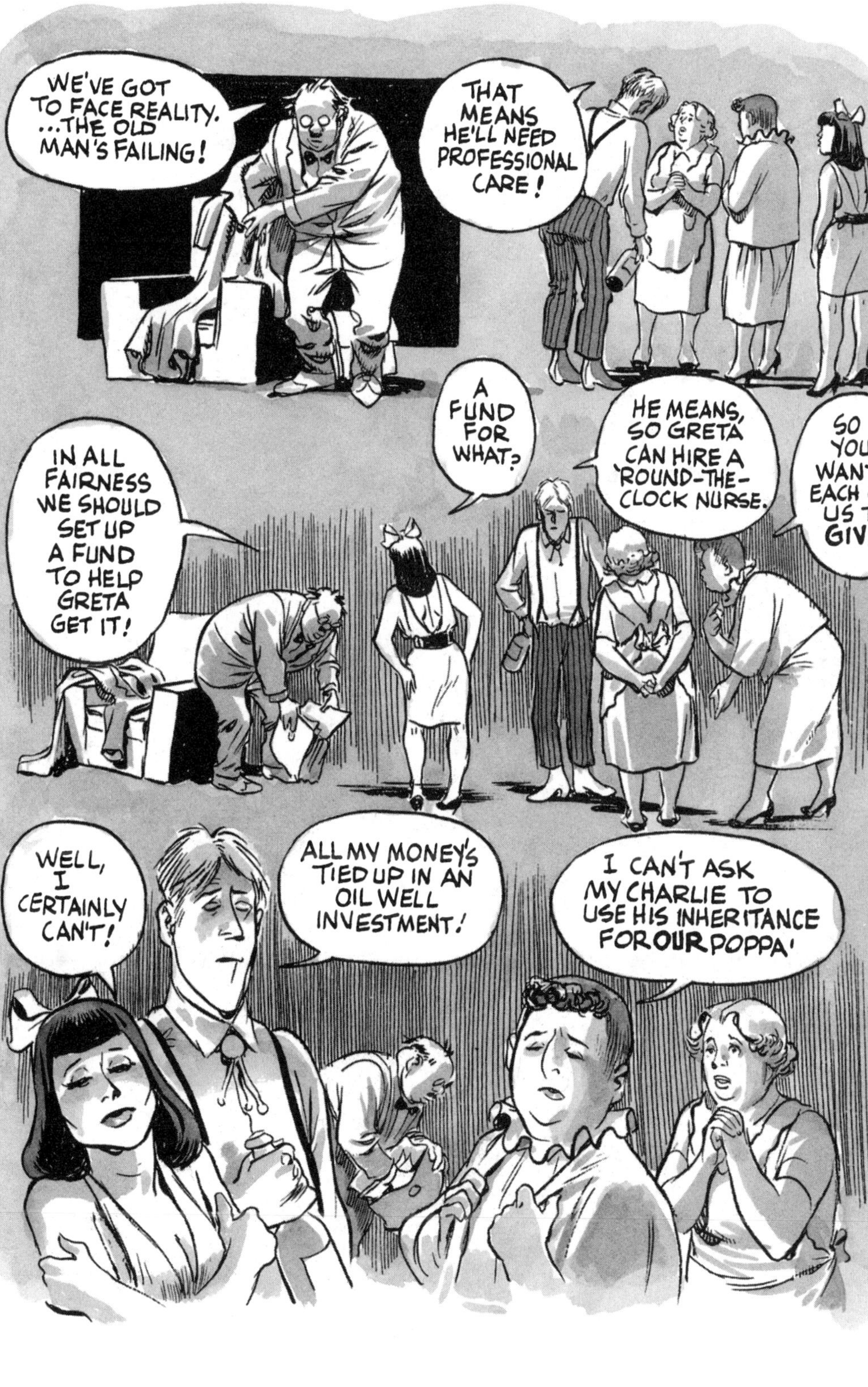
WE'VE GOT TO FACE REALITY. ...THE OLD MAN'S FAILING!
THAT MEANS HE'LL NEED PROFESSIONAL CARE!
IN ALL FAIRNESS WE SHOULD SET UP A FUND TO HELP GRETA GET IT!
A FUND FOR WHAT?
HE MEANS, SO GRETA CAN HIRE A 'ROUND-THE-CLOCK NURSE.
SO YOU WANT EACH OF US TO GIVE!
WELL, I CERTAINLY CAN'T!
ALL MY MONEY'S TIED UP IN AN OIL WELL INVESTMENT!
I CAN'T ASK MY CHARLIE TO USE HIS INHERITANCE FOR OUR POPPA!

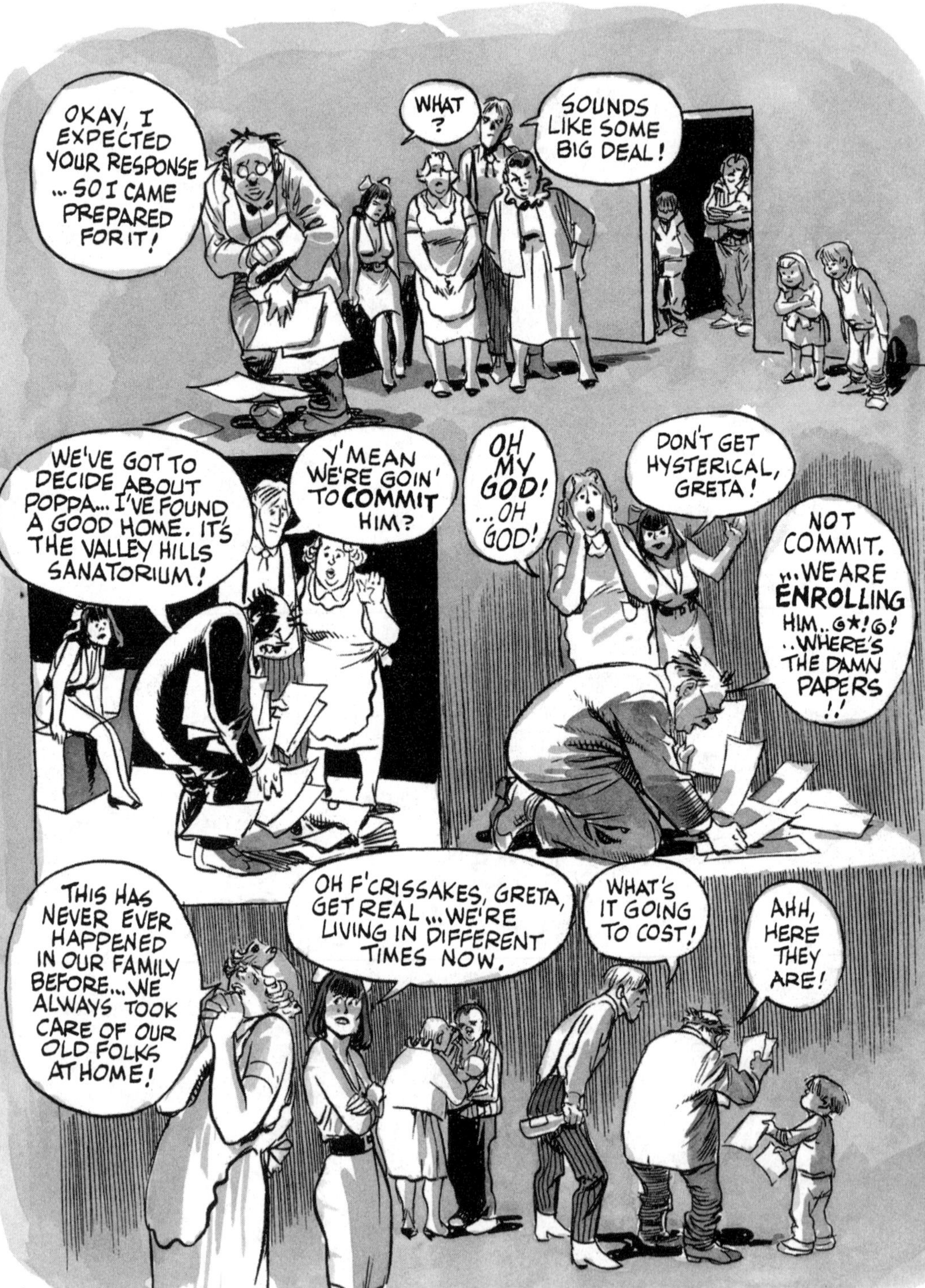
OKAY, I EXPECTED YOUR RESPONSE ... SO I CAME PREPARED FOR IT!
WHAT?
SOUNDS LIKE SOME BIG DEAL!
WE'VE GOT TO DECIDE ABOUT POPPA... I'VE FOUND A GOOD HOME. IT'S THE VALLEY HILLS SANATORIUM!
Y'MEAN WE'RE GOIN' TO COMMIT HIM?
OH MY GOD! ...OH GOD!
DON'T GET HYSTERICAL, GRETA!
NOT COMMIT. ...WE ARE ENROLLING HIM..@*!@! ..WHERE'S THE DAMN PAPERS!!
THIS HAS NEVER EVER HAPPENED IN OUR FAMILY BEFORE...WE ALWAYS TOOK CARE OF OUR OLD FOLKS AT HOME!
OH F'CRISSAKES, GRETA, GET REAL ...WE'RE LIVING IN DIFFERENT TIMES NOW.
WHAT'S IT GOING TO COST!
AHH, HERE THEY ARE!

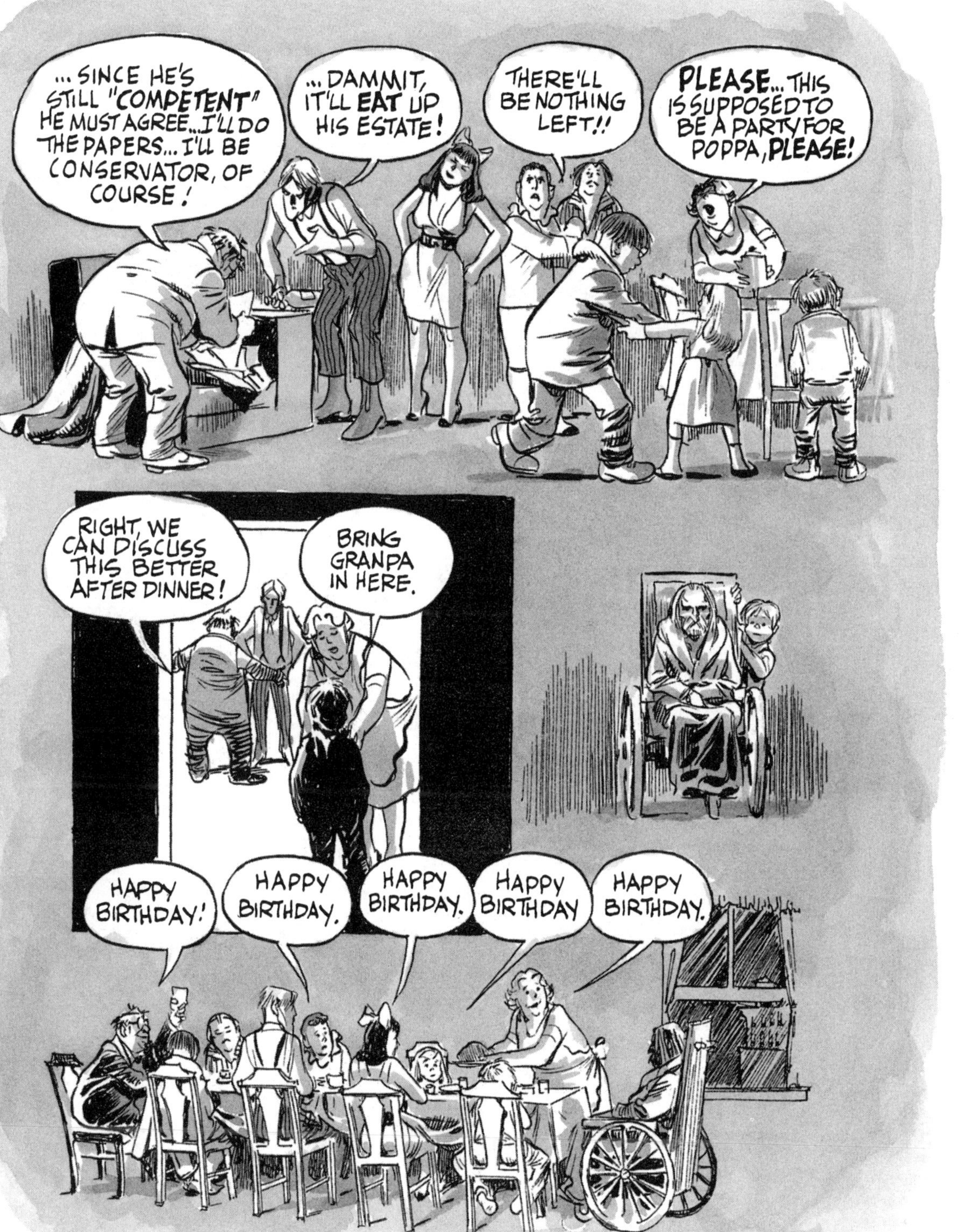
...SINCE HE'S STILL "COMPETENT" HE MUST AGREE...I'LL DO THE PAPERS...I'LL BE CONSERVATOR, OF COURSE!
...DAMMIT, IT'LL EAT UP HIS ESTATE!
THERE'LL BE NOTHING LEFT!!
PLEASE...THIS IS SUPPOSED TO BE A PARTY FOR POPPA, PLEASE!
RIGHT, WE CAN DISCUSS THIS BETTER AFTER DINNER!
BRING GRANPA IN HERE.
HAPPY BIRTHDAY!
HAPPY BIRTHDAY.
HAPPY BIRTHDAY.
HAPPY BIRTHDAY
HAPPY BIRTHDAY.

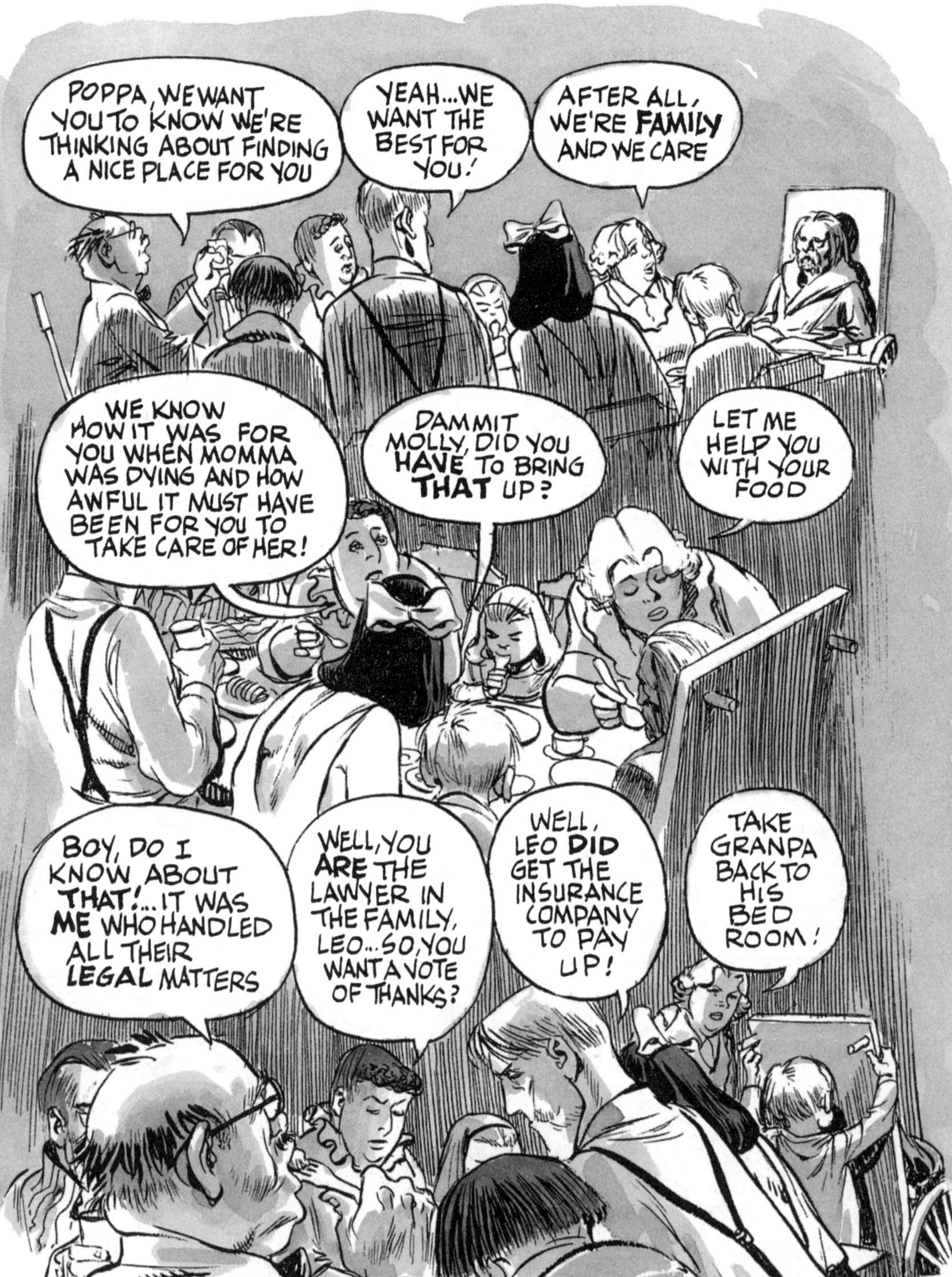
POPPA, WE WANT YOU TO KNOW WE'RE THINKING ABOUT FINDING A NICE PLACE FOR YOU
YEAH...WE WANT THE BEST FOR YOU!
AFTER ALL, WE'RE FAMILY AND WE CARE
WE KNOW HOW IT WAS FOR YOU WHEN MOMMA WAS DYING AND HOW AWFUL IT MUST HAVE BEEN FOR YOU TO TAKE CARE OF HER!
DAMMIT MOLLY, DID YOU HAVE TO BRING THAT UP?
LET ME HELP YOU WITH YOUR FOOD
BOY, DO I KNOW ABOUT THAT!...IT WAS ME WHO HANDLED ALL THEIR LEGAL MATTERS
WELL, YOU ARE THE LAWYER IN THE FAMILY, LEO...SO, YOU WANT A VOTE OF THANKS?
WELL, LEO DID GET THE INSURANCE COMPANY TO PAY UP!
TAKE GRANPA BACK TO HIS BED ROOM!

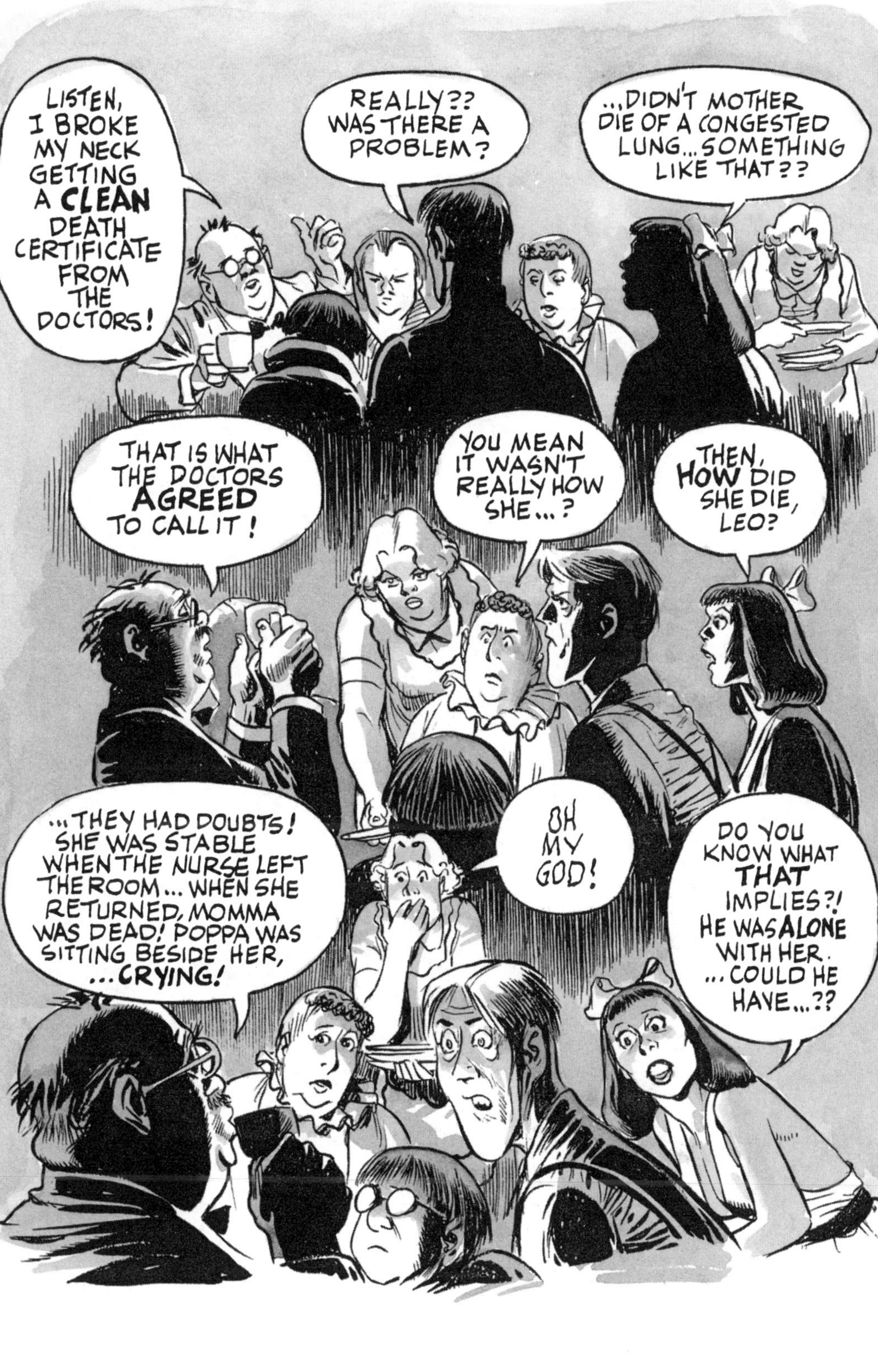
LISTEN, I BROKE MY NECK GETTING A CLEAN DEATH CERTIFICATE FROM THE DOCTORS!
REALLY?? WAS THERE A PROBLEM?
...DIDN'T MOTHER DIE OF A CONGESTED LUNG...SOMETHING LIKE THAT??
THAT IS WHAT THE DOCTORS AGREED TO CALL IT!
YOU MEAN IT WASN'T REALLY HOW SHE...?
THEN, HOW DID SHE DIE, LEO?
...THEY HAD DOUBTS! SHE WAS STABLE WHEN THE NURSE LEFT THE ROOM... WHEN SHE RETURNED, MOMMA WAS DEAD! POPPA WAS SITTING BESIDE HER, ...CRYING!
OH MY GOD!
DO YOU KNOW WHAT THAT IMPLIES?! HE WAS ALONE WITH HER. ...COULD HE HAVE...??

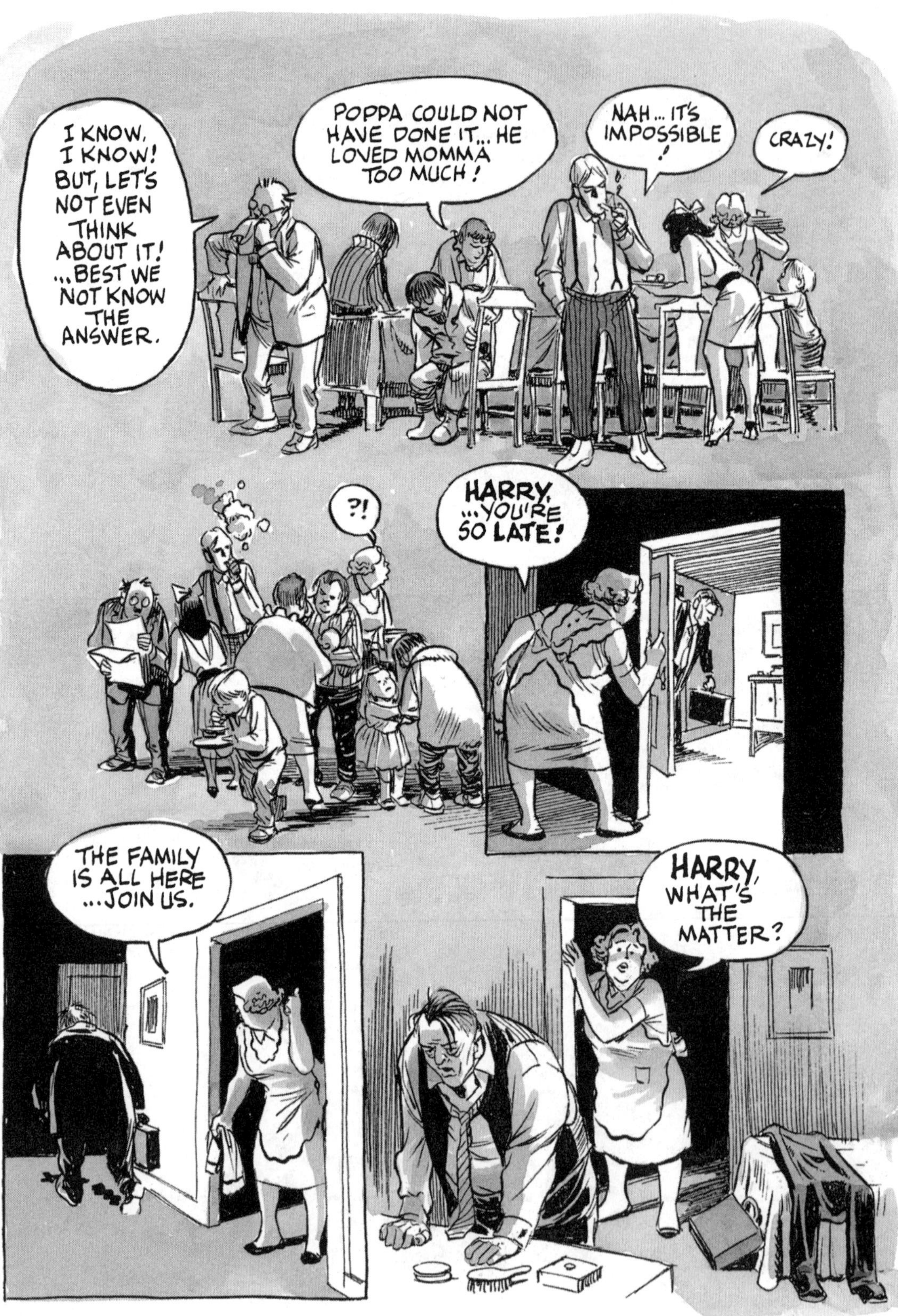
I KNOW, I KNOW! BUT, LET'S NOT EVEN THINK ABOUT IT! ...BEST WE NOT KNOW THE ANSWER.
POPPA COULD NOT HAVE DONE IT... HE LOVED MOMMA TOO MUCH!
NAH... IT'S IMPOSSIBLE!
CRAZY!
?!
HARRY, ...YOU'RE SO LATE!
THE FAMILY IS ALL HERE ...JOIN US.
HARRY, WHAT'S THE MATTER?

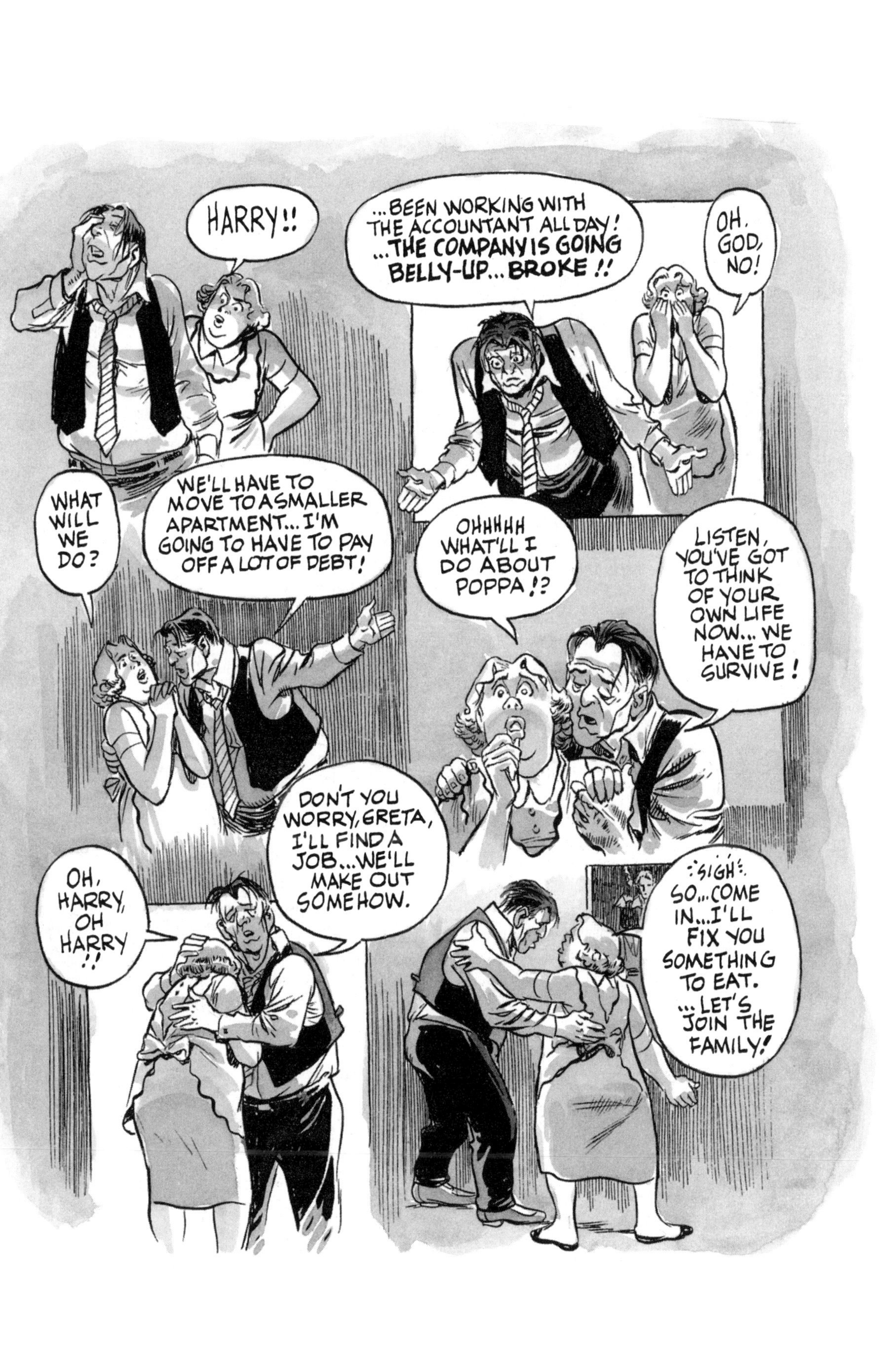
HARRY!!
...BEEN WORKING WITH THE ACCOUNTANT ALL DAY! ...THE COMPANY IS GOING BELLY-UP... BROKE!!
OH, GOD, NO!
WHAT WILL WE DO?
WE'LL HAVE TO MOVE TO A SMALLER APARTMENT... I'M GOING TO HAVE TO PAY OFF A LOT OF DEBT!
OHHHHH WHAT'LL I DO ABOUT POPPA!?
LISTEN, YOU'VE GOT TO THINK OF YOUR OWN LIFE NOW... WE HAVE TO SURVIVE!
OH, HARRY, OH HARRY!!
DON'T YOU WORRY, GRETA, I'LL FIND A JOB... WE'LL MAKE OUT SOMEHOW.
SIGH
SO... COME IN... I'LL FIX YOU SOMETHING TO EAT. ...LET'S JOIN THE FAMILY!

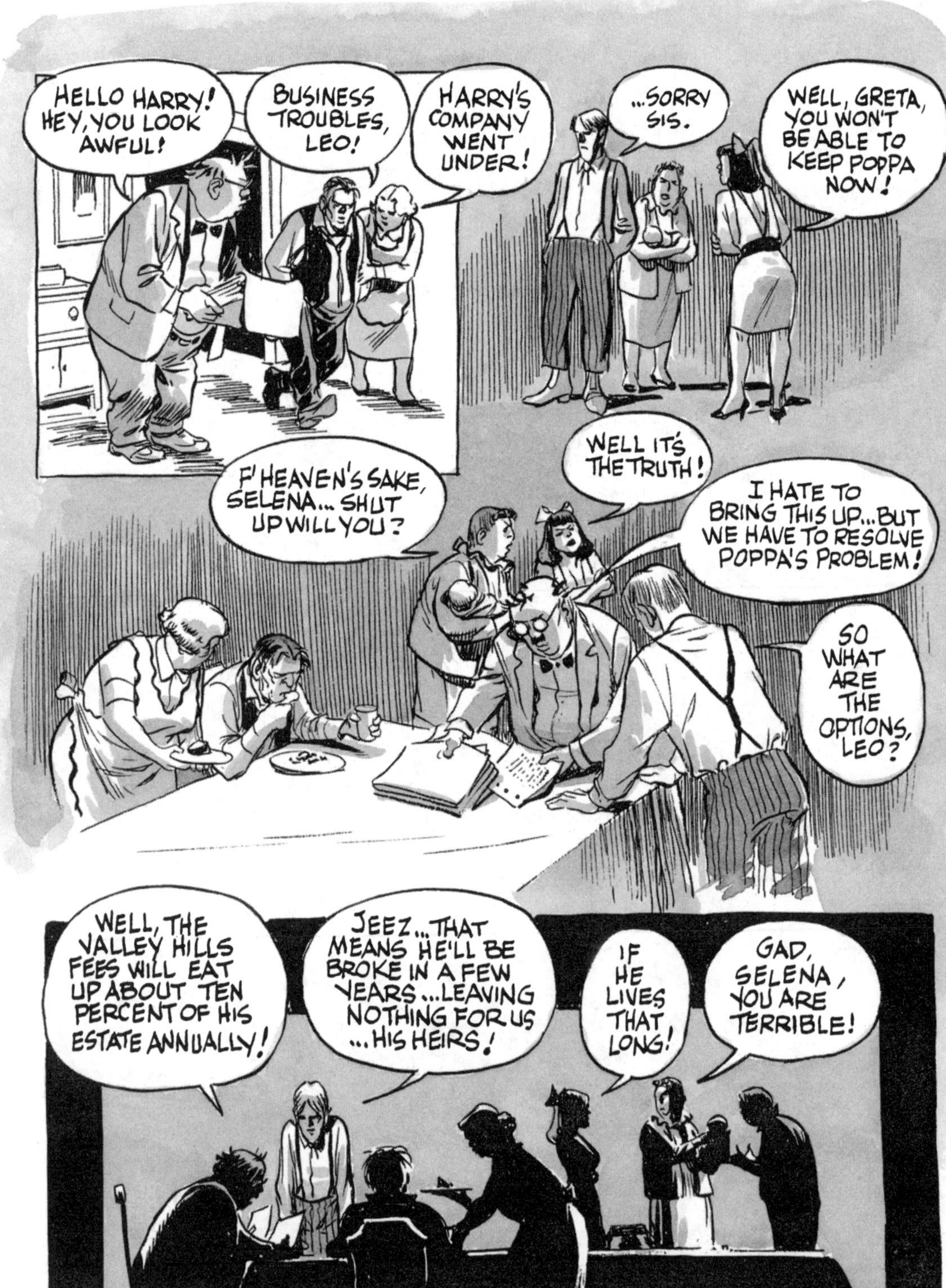
HELLO HARRY! HEY, YOU LOOK AWFUL!
BUSINESS TROUBLES, LEO!
HARRY'S COMPANY WENT UNDER!
...SORRY SIS.
WELL, GRETA, YOU WON'T BE ABLE TO KEEP POPPA NOW!
F' HEAVEN'S SAKE, SELENA... SHUT UP WILL YOU?
WELL IT'S THE TRUTH!
I HATE TO BRING THIS UP...BUT WE HAVE TO RESOLVE POPPA'S PROBLEM!
SO WHAT ARE THE OPTIONS, LEO?
WELL, THE VALLEY HILLS FEES WILL EAT UP ABOUT TEN PERCENT OF HIS ESTATE ANNUALLY!
JEEZ... THAT MEANS HE'LL BE BROKE IN A FEW YEARS ...LEAVING NOTHING FOR US ...HIS HEIRS!
IF HE LIVES THAT LONG!
GAD, SELENA, YOU ARE TERRIBLE!

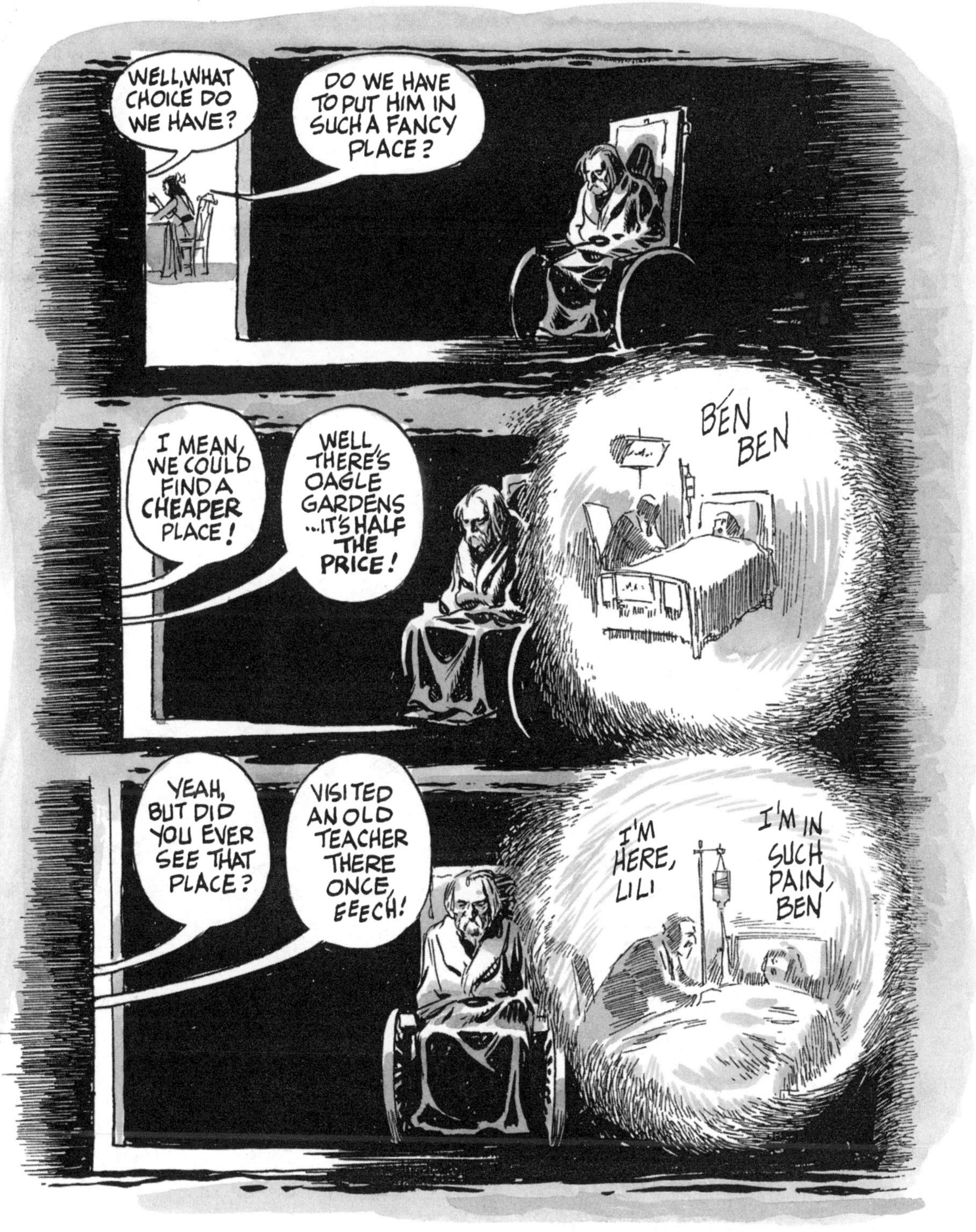
WELL, WHAT CHOICE DO WE HAVE?
DO WE HAVE TO PUT HIM IN SUCH A FANCY PLACE?
I MEAN, WE COULD FIND A CHEAPER PLACE!
WELL, THERE'S OAGLE GARDENS ...IT'S HALF THE PRICE!
BEN BEN
YEAH, BUT DID YOU EVER SEE THAT PLACE?
VISITED AN OLD TEACHER THERE ONCE, EEECH!
I'M HERE, LILI
I'M IN SUCH PAIN, BEN

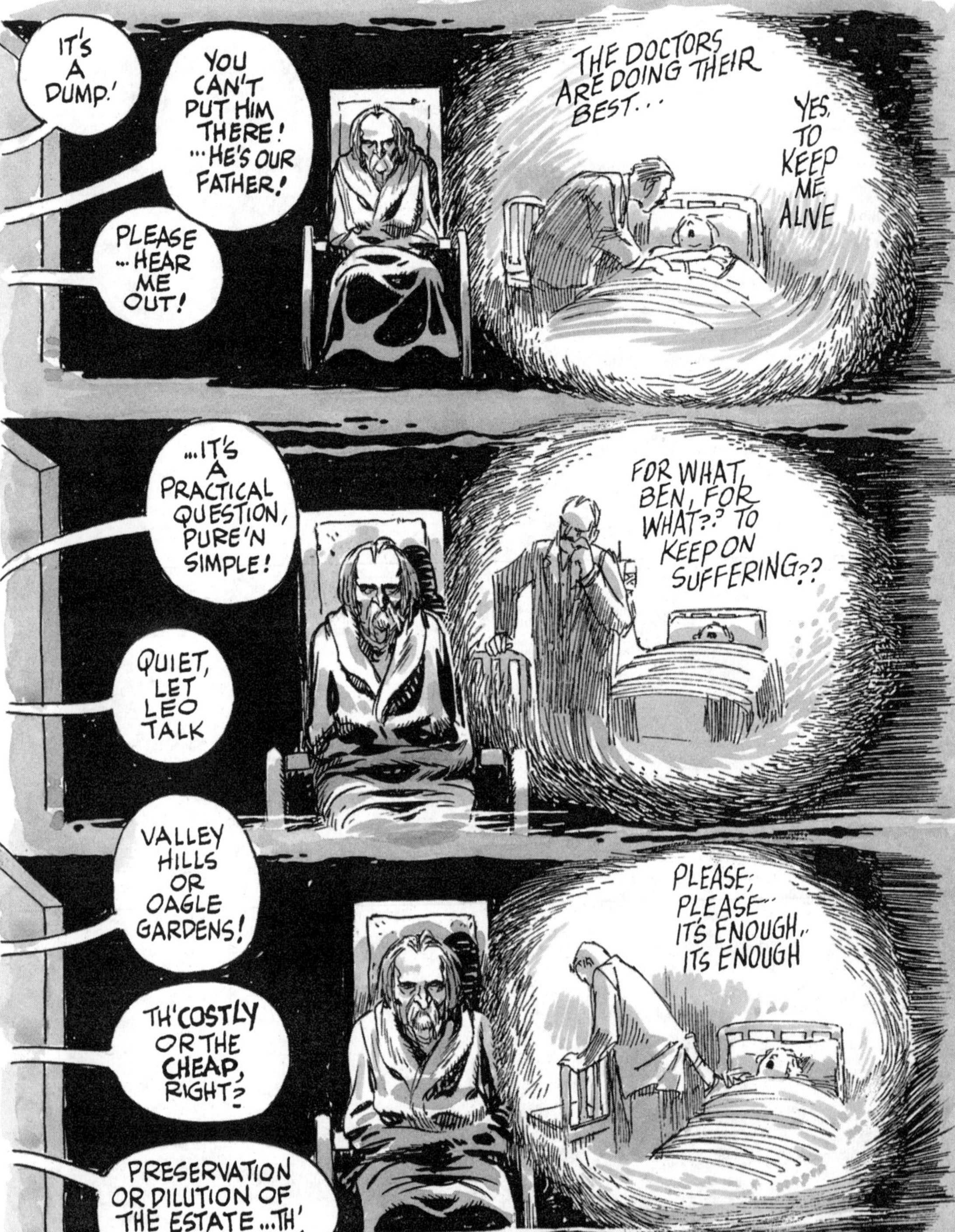
IT'S A DUMP!
YOU CAN'T PUT HIM THERE! ...HE'S OUR FATHER!
PLEASE ...HEAR ME OUT!
THE DOCTORS ARE DOING THEIR BEST...
YES, TO KEEP ME ALIVE
...IT'S A PRACTICAL QUESTION, PURE'N SIMPLE!
QUIET, LET LEO TALK
FOR WHAT, BEN, FOR WHAT?? TO KEEP ON SUFFERING??
VALLEY HILLS OR OAGLE GARDENS!
TH' COSTLY OR THE CHEAP, RIGHT?
PRESERVATION OR DILUTION OF THE ESTATE ...TH' BOTTOM LINE!
PLEASE, PLEASE... IT'S ENOUGH.. IT'S ENOUGH

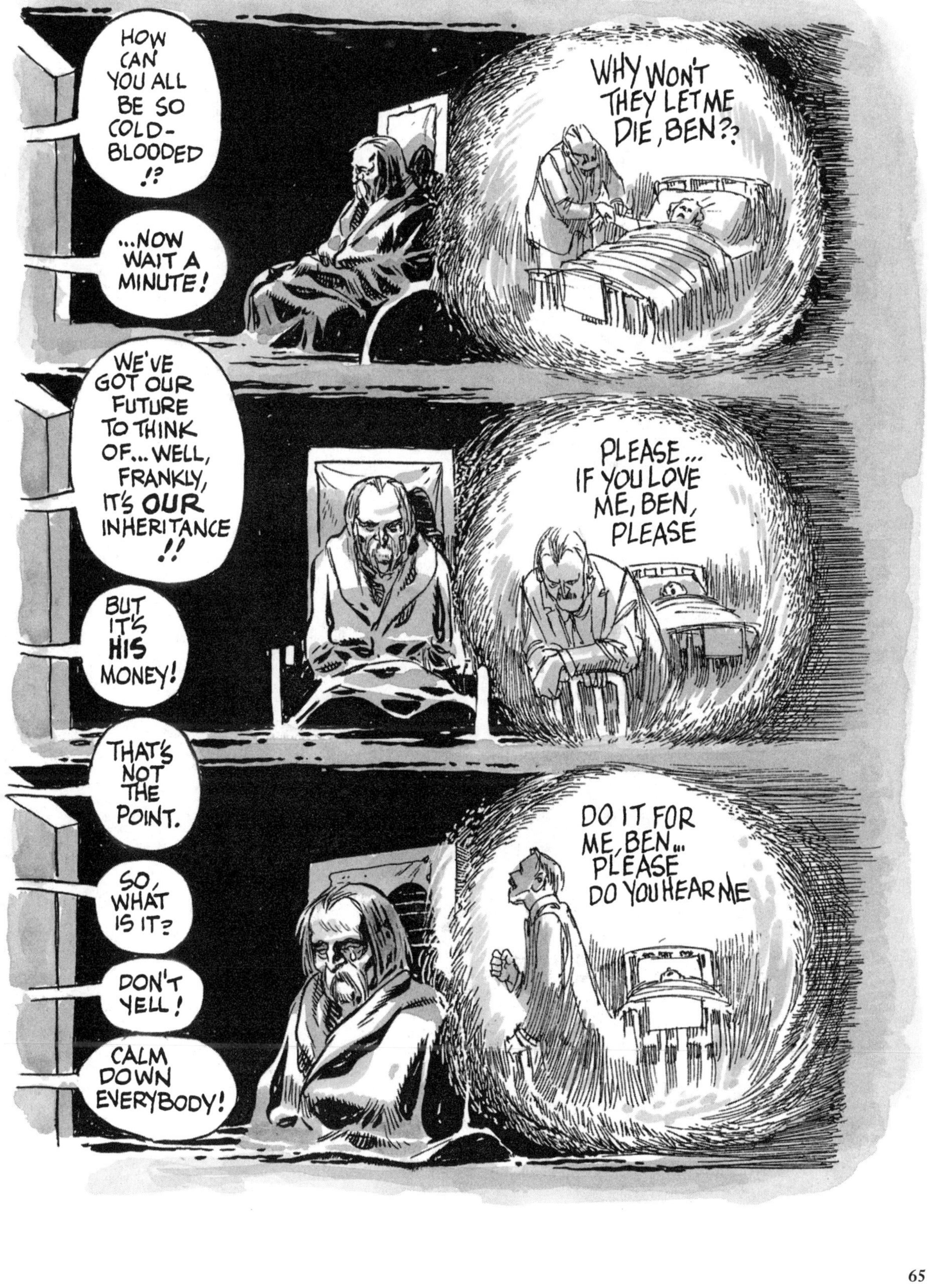
HOW CAN YOU ALL BE SO COLD-BLOODED !?
WHY WON'T THEY LET ME DIE, BEN??
...NOW WAIT A MINUTE!
WE'VE GOT OUR FUTURE TO THINK OF... WELL, FRANKLY, IT'S OUR INHERITANCE !!
PLEASE... IF YOU LOVE ME, BEN, PLEASE
BUT IT'S HIS MONEY!
THAT'S NOT THE POINT.
DO IT FOR ME, BEN... PLEASE DO YOU HEAR ME
SO, WHAT IS IT?
DON'T YELL!
CALM DOWN EVERYBODY!

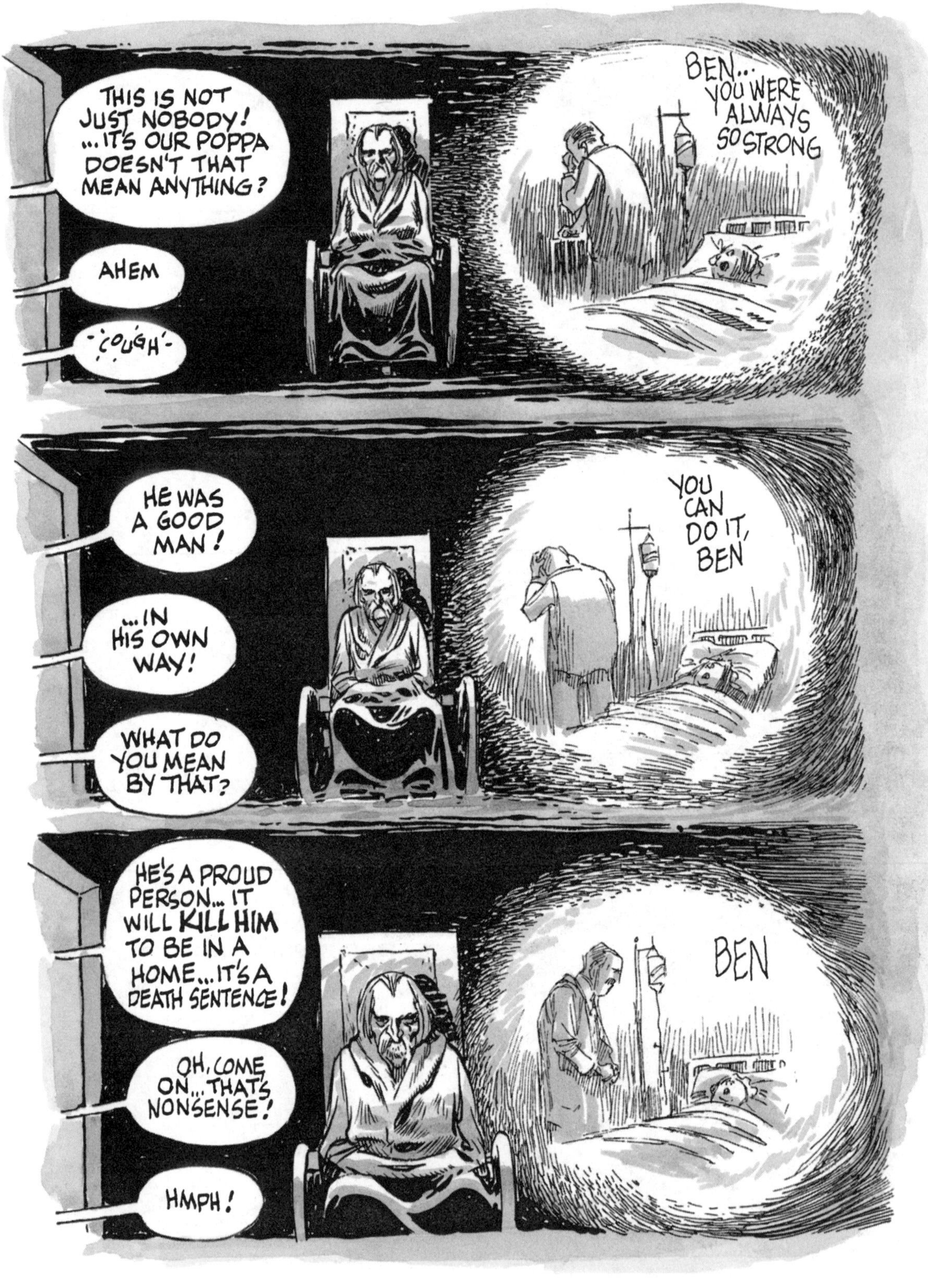
THIS IS NOT JUST NOBODY! ...IT'S OUR POPPA DOESN'T THAT MEAN ANYTHING?
AHEM
-COUGH-
BEN... YOU WERE ALWAYS SO STRONG
HE WAS A GOOD MAN!
...IN HIS OWN WAY!
WHAT DO YOU MEAN BY THAT?
YOU CAN DO IT, BEN
HE'S A PROUD PERSON... IT WILL KILL HIM TO BE IN A HOME...IT'S A DEATH SENTENCE!
OH, COME ON...THAT'S NONSENSE!
HMPH!
BEN

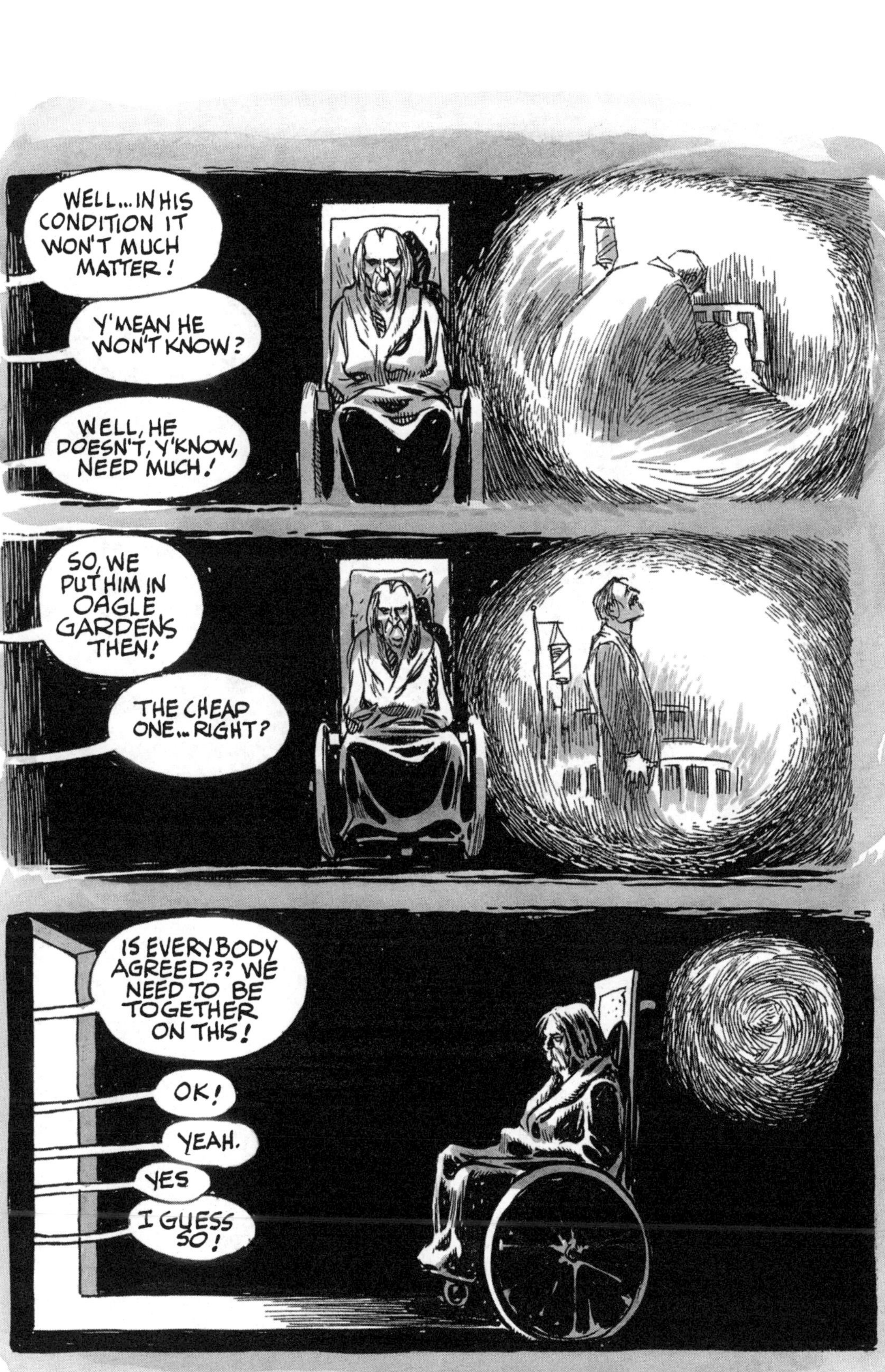
WELL... IN HIS CONDITION IT WON'T MUCH MATTER!
Y'MEAN HE WON'T KNOW?
WELL, HE DOESN'T, Y'KNOW, NEED MUCH!
SO, WE PUT HIM IN OAGLE GARDENS THEN!
THE CHEAP ONE.. RIGHT?
IS EVERYBODY AGREED?? WE NEED TO BE TOGETHER ON THIS!
OK!
YEAH.
YES
I GUESS SO!

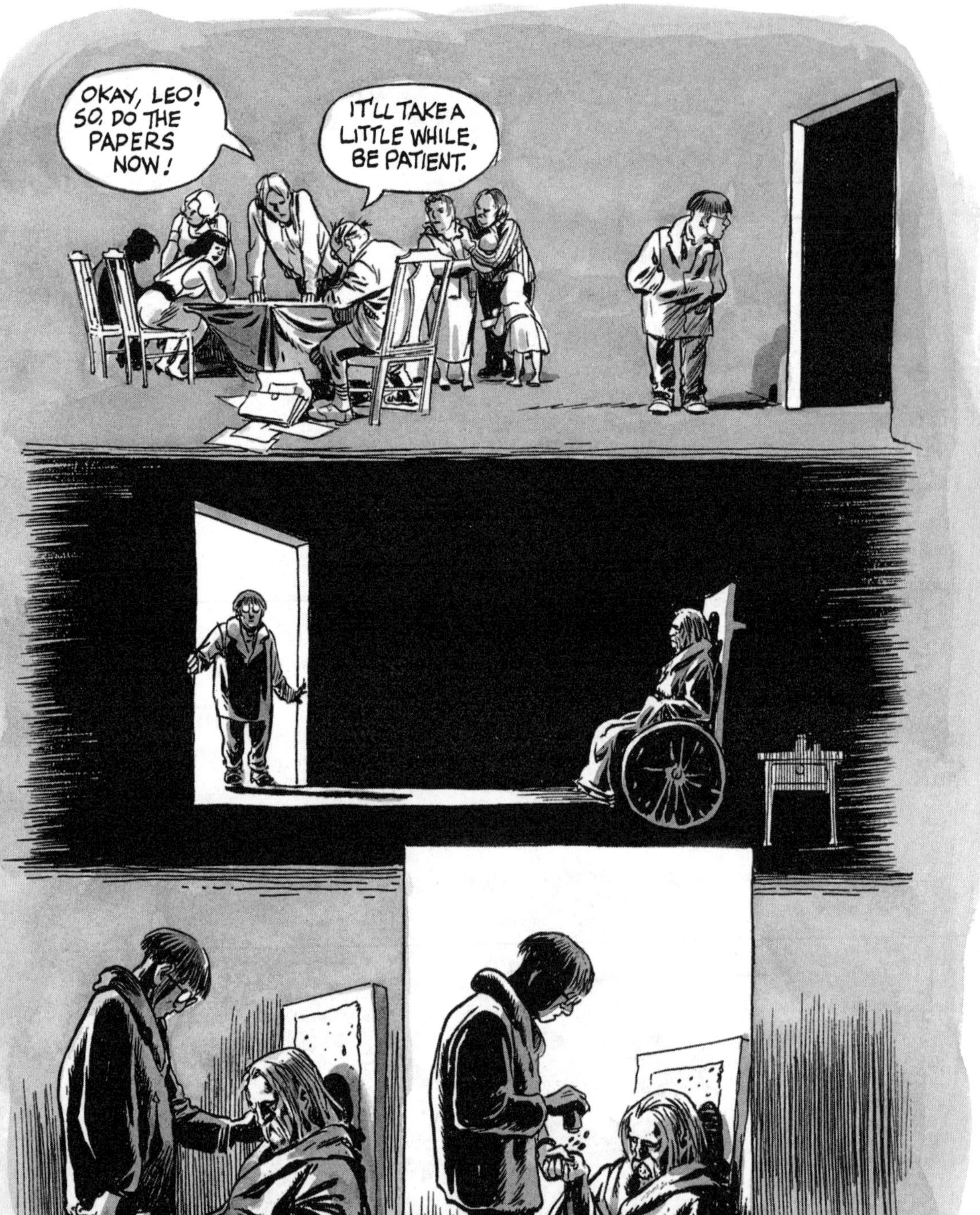
OKAY, LEO! SO, DO THE PAPERS NOW!
IT'LL TAKE A LITTLE WHILE. BE PATIENT.

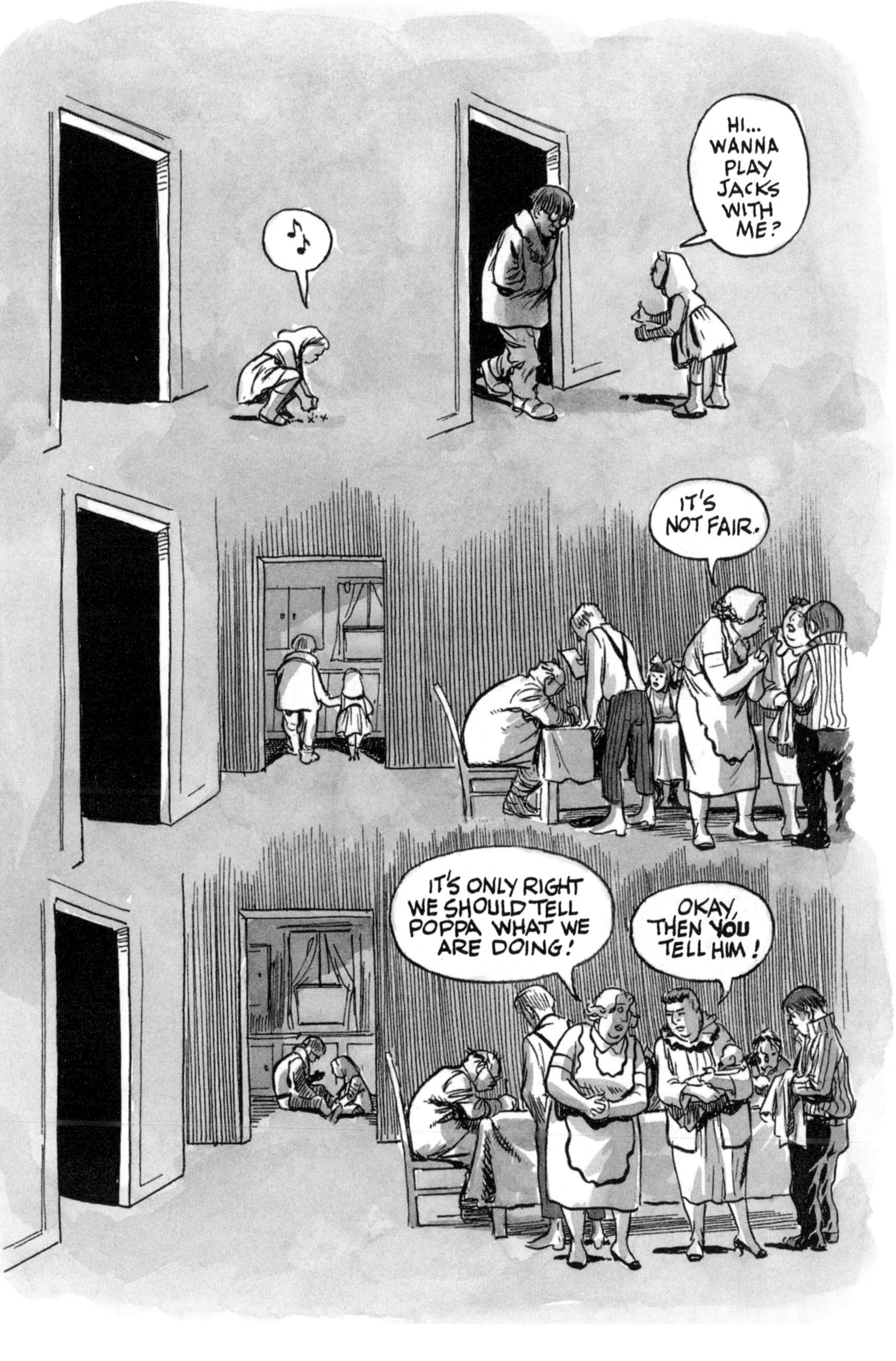
HI... WANNA PLAY JACKS WITH ME?
IT'S NOT FAIR.
IT'S ONLY RIGHT WE SHOULD TELL POPPA WHAT WE ARE DOING!
OKAY, THEN YOU TELL HIM!

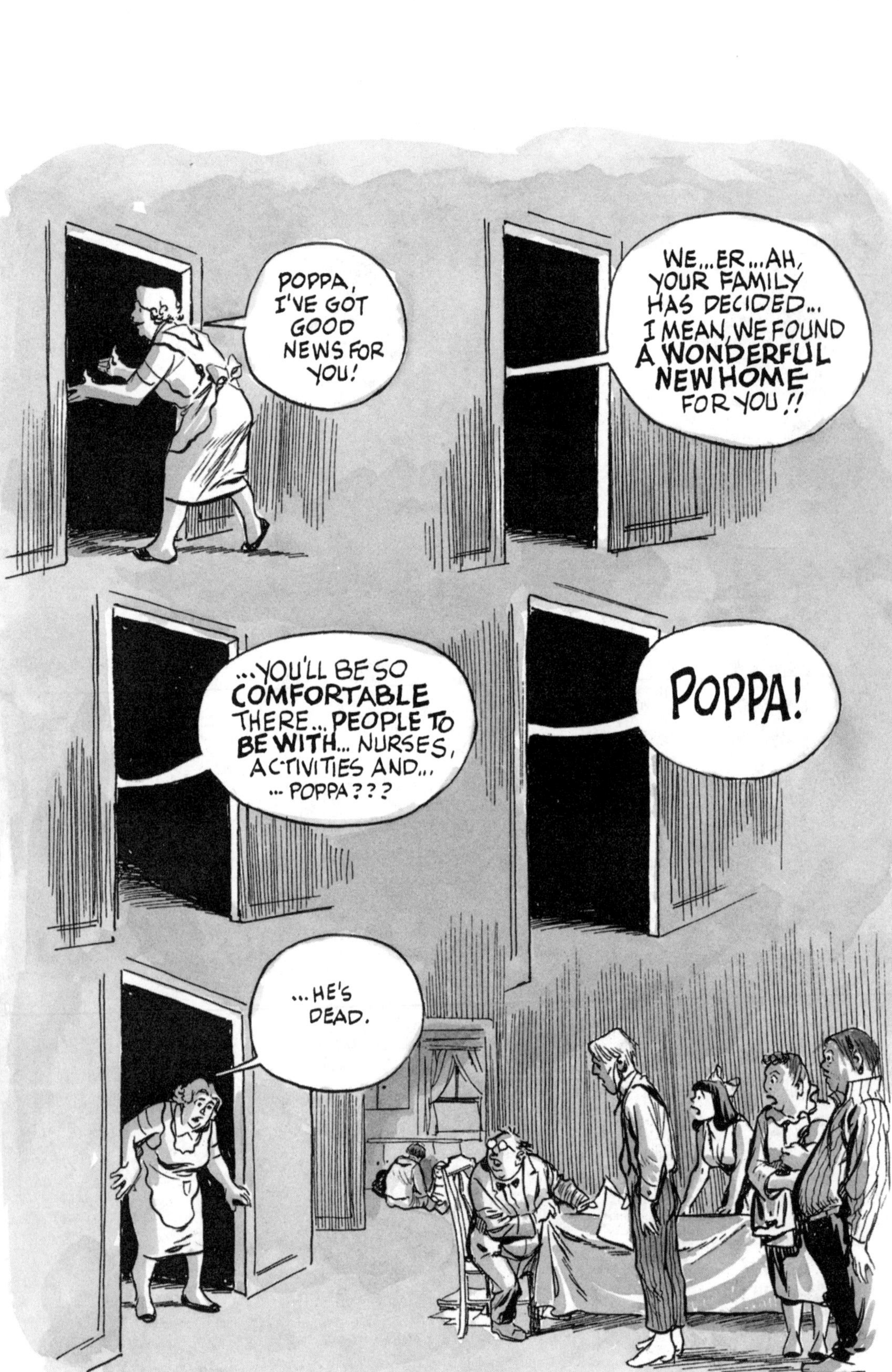
POPPA, I'VE GOT GOOD NEWS FOR YOU!
WE...ER...AH, YOUR FAMILY HAS DECIDED... I MEAN, WE FOUND A WONDERFUL NEW HOME FOR YOU!!
...YOU'LL BE SO COMFORTABLE THERE... PEOPLE TO BE WITH... NURSES, ACTIVITIES AND... ...POPPA???
POPPA!
...HE'S DEAD.

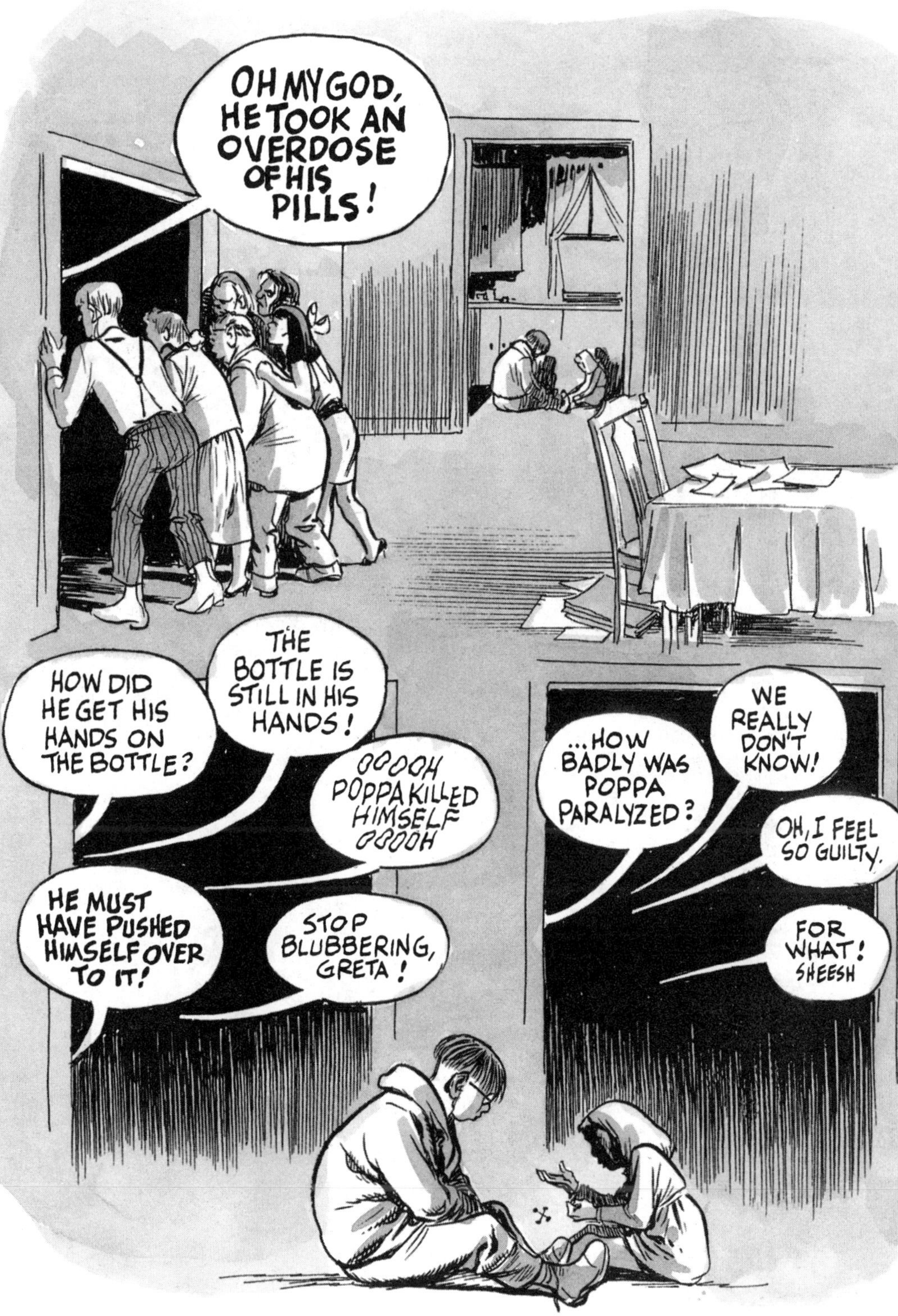
OH MY GOD, HE TOOK AN OVERDOSE OF HIS PILLS!
HOW DID HE GET HIS HANDS ON THE BOTTLE?
THE BOTTLE IS STILL IN HIS HANDS!
OOOOH POPPA KILLED HIMSELF OOOOH
HE MUST HAVE PUSHED HIMSELF OVER TO IT!
STOP BLUBBERING, GRETA!
...HOW BADLY WAS POPPA PARALYZED?
WE REALLY DON'T KNOW!
OH, I FEEL SO GUILTY.
FOR WHAT! SHEESH

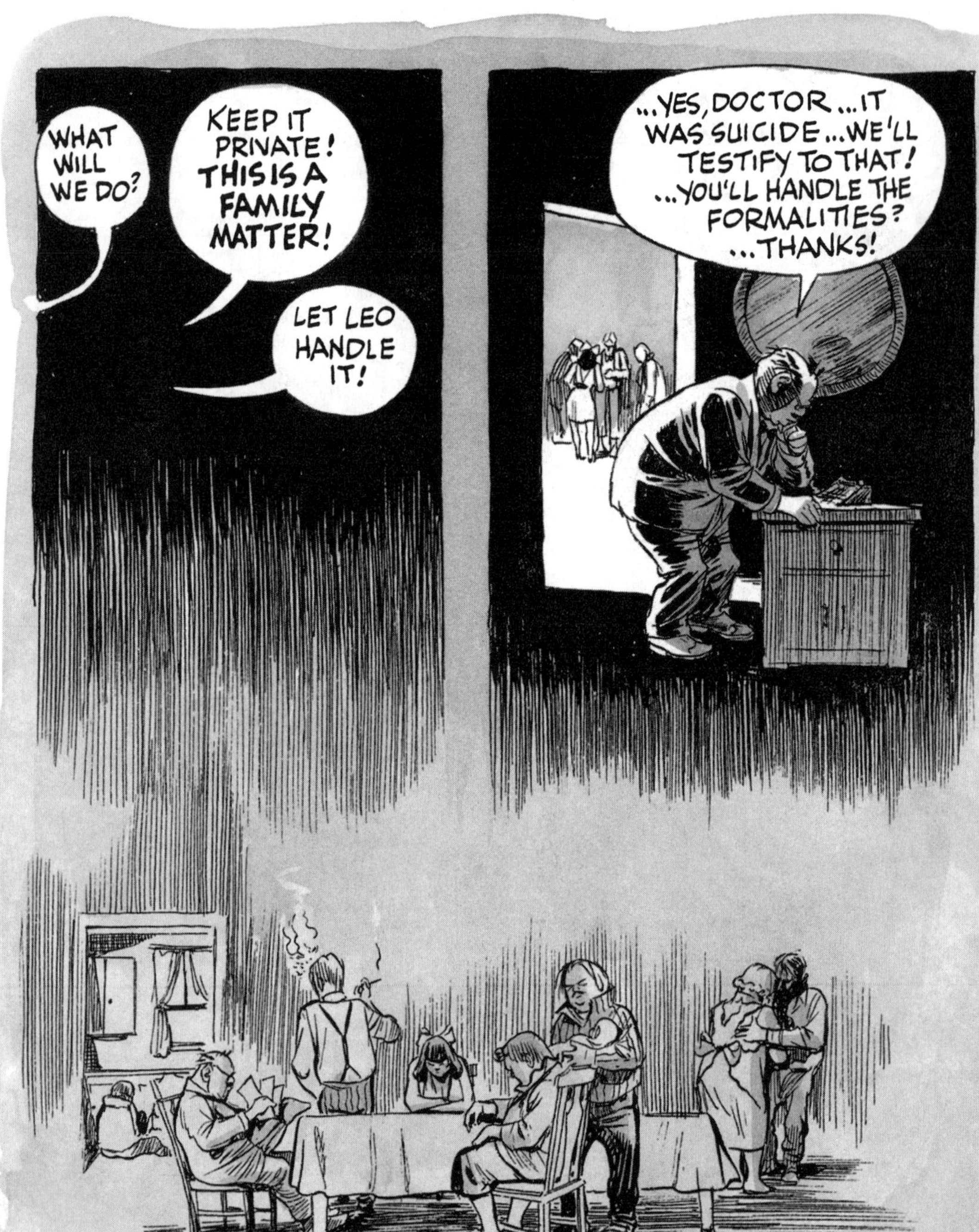
WHAT WILL WE DO?
KEEP IT PRIVATE! THIS IS A FAMILY MATTER!
LET LEO HANDLE IT!
...YES, DOCTOR ...IT WAS SUICIDE ...WE'LL TESTIFY TO THAT! ...YOU'LL HANDLE THE FORMALITIES? ...THANKS!

About the Author

Will Eisner (1917–2005) is universally acknowledged as one of the great masters of comic book art, beginning as a teenager during the birth of the comic book industry in the mid-1930s. After a successful career as a packager of comic books for various publishers, he created a groundbreaking weekly newspaper comic book insert, *The Spirit*, which was syndicated worldwide for a dozen years and influenced countless other cartoonists, including Frank Miller, who wrote and directed the major motion picture based on it. In 1952, Eisner devoted himself to the then still nascent field of educational comics. Among these projects was *P*S*, a monthly technical manual utilizing comics, published by the United States Army for over two decades, and comics-based teaching material for schools. In the mid-1970s, Eisner returned to his first love, storytelling with sequential art. In 1978, he wrote and drew the pioneering graphic novel *A Contract With God*. He went on to create another twenty celebrated graphic novels. The Eisners, the comics industry's annual awards for excellence (equivalent to the Oscars in film), are named in his honor.